This book is a work of fiction imagination. All names, characters, events, places, products etc. have been used for this fictional purpose. If, by chance, they or it resembles someone or something; living or dead, it is by coincidence. All scriptures are taken from the Bible and is not the work of the author.

*** Although this is Christian Fiction, there is some foul language included. ***

Published by: Twins Write 2 Publishing

© 2021 by Lakisha Johnson

Wondah

Finding strength to overcome the pain

Dedication

This book is dedicated to those of you who have found yourself going through a divorce. Whether it was made final or you worked through it, the journey of divorce is hard. It leaves you grieving the death of what you thought would last.

While this book may not give you the full answer, I pray it gives you hope because I'm praying for you. I'm praying you find the right methods to cope. I'm praying you find the right methods to heal. I'm praying you don't forsake love. I'm praying you don't forget you.

Trust God through your process.

My Thanks

I'll always begin by thanking God. It's Him who believes enough in who He created to trust me with this gift. This is why, even when its hard and it doesn't pay off like I expect, I never give up. I accept this gift every day and I proudly and unapologetically serve God through it.

To my family; my husbae Willie, children, mom, sisters, brothers—the entire family; know I love each of you for supporting me, release after release.

A special shout out to my sister Laquisha and my girl, Shakendria and Ms. Lillie Brown for helping me to ensure I craft great books.

To each of you who support Lakisha, the PreacHER, Author and Blogger ... THANK YOU! I wouldn't be who I am without supporters like you who purchase, download, recommend and review my books. Please, don't stop believing in me.

Disclaimer

Trigger Warning: Wondah's story is one of divorce, anger, pain and borderline depression. Reading her story may trigger unresolved emotions and pain for you. Guard yourself and your heart. If this means you are unable to read this, I understand and pray one of my other books will be a better fit.

Here's the link to my website. www.authorlakishajohnson.com

Also, this is a work of Christian Fiction and within this book is prayers, scriptures and sermons. There's also cursing because we're dealing with the raw emotions of anger. Again, if these are the kinds of things you don't like to read and will cause you to leave a low review, I implore you to return this book.

For me, this isn't simply writing another book, it's ministry and sometimes ministry isn't confined to tradition. Sometimes, we have to meet people where they are and unfortunately, it may be a place of darkness and pain. If you're deciding to read on, HAPPY READING!

Lakisha

Wondah

Finding strength to overcome the pain

Chapter 1

"Eve, do you believe your husband has changed?"

She looks at him and he smiles.

"No," she flatly responds never blinking and his smile quickly fading. "I think he's doing what I need him to do."

"Then why are we here?" Nathan, her husband angrily asks. "We've been doing this dance for over two months and you still don't believe me. What's the point?"

"Nathan, calm down." I tell him. "Forgiveness takes time."

"I've given her time."

"No, bastard, you've given me trust issues. How dare you expect me to forget you were having an affair with an ex who's now carrying your child. An ex you claimed to hate and yet, you found time to slip between her legs every chance you got. You promised to be faithful to me and," she pauses. "Dr. Jennings, I thought I could forgive him and work on our marriage, but I can't. I love Nathan however staying with him means I have to help raise the product of his infidelity and this was never part of the vows I took. Yeah, um we're done, and this marriage is over."

"After eleven years," Nathan barks.

"The length of our marriage shouldn't be the deciding factor on whether I stay because it sure in hell didn't stop you from cheating. So, yes after eleven years I'm finally giving you what you've silently been asking for." She stands and grabs her purse. "Your freedom. Dr. Jennings, thank you for your time and help, but we won't be needing your services anymore."

She walks out. I look at Nathan who's staring at the door.

"Really dude."

He turns to me with his forehead creased.

"You allowed your wife, whom you claim to love and want, to walk out of here and you never got up to stop or go after her."

"She said our marriage is over."

I shake my head. Leaning forward, I clasp my hands in my lap.

"Your wife is hurt because you cheated on her, broke the vows you declared before God and your church while destroying her trust in you and love. Yes, she said it was over, and no matter if it is over or not, you owe it to her to at least fight for her. Even if she rejects you, going after her shows you still respect her enough to care about her feelings. She's in this place of hurt because of you."

"I know, but what else am I supposed to do? She won't let me in after I've apologized over and over. Dr. Jennings, I didn't set out to cheat on my wife. I love her, and I made a mistake."

I chuckle and sit back. "You make a mistake when you grab cottage cheese when you meant to get sour cream because the packaging is similar. A mistake is leaving the house with one brown shoe and the other is black because you didn't turn the light on. Cheating is a choice. Why did you cheat?"

"I don't know."

"Sure, you do. Nathan, God has given us common sense to know why we do things. However, we've gotten great at using I don't know as an excuse. You knew why each time you chose to cheat. Why did you cheat on your wife?" I ask again.

He pauses. "Lana was convenient and comfortable. With her I didn't have to be husband, provider or fixer. She was an escape from everything I have going on in my life."

"An escape? Dude, an escape is taking a vacation. What you did was adultery and if you truly feel like cheating on your wife is the escape you needed from a marriage you chose to be in, you don't deserve to be husband or provider and you damn sure don't deserve Eve."

"I know," he sighs. "I realized how stupid the words sounded when they left my mouth. I'm going to apologize to Eve again, but this time I'm letting her go because I don't deserve her. I can only pray I didn't destroy her chance at real love."

"You don't hold that much power, but good luck with everything."

When he leaves, I get up and go over to my desk stopping the video. I save it to my iCloud before making a few notes and shutting the computer down.

"Happy Birthday to you," Asha, my assistant sings with a cupcake and one candle after bursting through the door. "Since you're on vacation tomorrow and next week, I couldn't allow you to leave without celebrating your birthday. You only turn 50 once."

I stand and blow out the candle.

"Thank you, A. I really appreciate this."

She hands me a box. I open it to find a customized wine bottle sleeve along with my favorite wine. "Asha, this is beautiful, and you know I'm about to enjoy this wine with my husbae, tonight." I dance.

"Alright now, don't blame me when you end up pregnant at 50," she laughs.

"Baby, I've been spayed for years now." I joke referring to the hysterectomy I had six years ago. "Ain't nothing else coming out of this who-ha, but I won't be mad at him for putting something in."

She laughs. "Just nasty. Get out of here and enjoy your vacation."

Chapter 2

I roll over stretching my hands over my head with a huge smile on my face. I look over at the empty wine glasses and bottle along with a strawberry shortcake candle and few toys Harvey and I used to set the mood last night while bringing in my birthday. I excitedly kick my legs because I'm 50.

"Happy birthday to me." I squeal. After a few minutes, I throw the comforter back and kneel beside the bed.

"Lord, thank you for this day. You've allowed me to see fifty years on Earth and for this I am grateful. Please keep your hands on me, allowing this next part of my journey to be more bless than the first. Guide me, fill me and lead me in the direction of my life's assignment even if I have to disconnect from what I'm comfortable with. Fifty biblically means the relationship to the coming of God's Holy Spirit, so whatever you have for me next, don't let me miss it. Whatever this next part of life is for me, give me grace to accomplish and agree with it. In your name I pray, amen."

I stay there a few more minutes, letting the spirit of God settle within me. Afterwards, I shower and dress. Coming out of the bedroom, the sounds of raised voices from the kitchen quickens my steps. Stopping at the door, I see my husband and daughter in a heated argument. When she pushes him, I step forward.

"Woah, what's going on?" I ask.

"Why didn't you tell me?" Haven screams in my direction with tears streaming down her face.

"Tell you what?" I question confused. "What's going on?"

She looks at her dad.

"Harvey?" I turn to my husband who runs a hand over his face.

"I came home thinking we were celebrating your birthday and instead dad says you're getting a divorce. Why wouldn't you tell me?"

I chuckle before quickly realizing she's serious. I look from her to him. He's standing there, his face void of emotion. When he moves away from the counter, I see a brown envelope with his ring on top.

"You didn't know?" Haven finally figures out. "Wow."

"Harvey?"

"Wondah, I'm sorry to do this on your birthday, but it had to be done because well, I've put it off long enough and I didn't want to give you the wrong impression."

"The wrong impression. What the hell does that mean?"

He shrugs. "A copy of the divorce papers is there." He points. "You can have your attorney look over them."

I walk over and rip the envelope open. Scanning through it, it's clear Harvey only wants to be free of this marriage because all he's asking for is his 401k, car and clothes.

"You can keep the house, the money in the checking and savings accounts and I've already had my name removed from your practice."

"Gee thanks. Who knew a husband could give you what's already yours." I sarcastically state.

"As I said, you can have your attorney look over everything, but you'll find I've been more than fair."

"No need." I cut him off before snatching open the junk drawer searching for a pen.

"You don't have to sign them, they're not the official documents." He states, and I ignore him.

"That's it?" Haven questions me. "You're not going to say anything?"

"Nope. It's obvious there's nothing else to say. His mind is made up and I refuse to fight for a punk who was going to leave divorce papers for his wife of twenty-seven years like this marriage or me has meant nothing."

"This isn't what I'm doing," he barks.

"Then what are you doing coward? From my viewpoint, you were going to let me wake up and find these papers without an explanation or conversation." I snap.

"I didn't want to argue, and I knew we would."

"You didn't want to argue," Haven laughs. "Are you freaking serious? You have divorce papers dad and it's clear this isn't something you and mom discussed, so what the fuc—

"Haven," he cuts her off. "I know you're upset but this is between me and your mother."

"Like hell it is." She screams at him. "This affects all three of us and you don't get to decide you want out without hearing what we have to say. You owe us an explanation."

He sighs. "I'm sorry to spring this on y'all and you're right, I should have said something sooner, but there was never a right time. It's not like I came up with this overnight, I've been toiling for the last year."

"A year?" Haven spats stepping towards him. I touch her arm to stop her.

I chuckle. "You've been contemplating divorce for a year? Hmm, that's strange because we took a trip to Hawaii last year and there was no mention of a divorce. At the lake for Labor Day, there was nothing implied. When we took new family photos at Christmas, I don't recall it being brought up. Oh, wait it had to be before we bought new rings three months ago for our anniversary but, nope. Damn. Either I've been living in an alternate universe or you're full of shit." I say flipping through the papers again. "And according to these documents, we have irreconcilable differences. What are they?"

He rolls his eyes.

I move towards him and if it was possible, smoke would be coming out of my ears. "You smug motherfucker. You're standing in the house we built, looking me in the face without emotions like we met yesterday. The same face you looked in last night while we made love knowing you were planning to serve me with divorce papers ON MY FREAKING BIRTHDAY." I seethe. Taking a step back, I laugh shaking my head. "I have to give it to you, you had me fooled because I never saw this coming. However, you better be glad your daughter is here, or this could very well be a crime scene."

"I'm sorry."

"That's the first honest thing you've said." Haven scoffs. "You're definitely sorry."

"I only hope you never get the karma you deserve and allow me to leave you with the same words from Maddie Townsend in Sweet Magnolias. You aren't worth the skin God spent to wrap your bones in and you best pray He doesn't regret His investment in you as much as I regret mine." I press the papers into his chest. "Divorce granted. Get your shit out of my house."

I turn to walk away, quickly changing my mind and instead punching him twice in the face before he can react.

"Now, you can get your shit out of my house."

Haven follows me into the bedroom as I shake the pain from my hand.

"Mom."

I keep walking.

"Mom," she yells.

"What?" she jumps from the forcefulness of my voice. "I'm sorry. I don't know what you want me to say or do Haven. I was blindsided as much as you were but there's nothing I can do. It's obvious our marriage has been over, I only wish he'd told me."

I slump on the bed.

"I'm sorry," she cries, and I reach out my hand to her.

"You have nothing to apologize for and neither are we going to sit around sulking over the decisions of a grown man. He wants out, I'm giving it to him. Life goes on. How about we get breakfast? It is my birthday after all."

She leans her head on my shoulder.

"You don't have to be strong for me." She tells me.

"No, I have to be strong for me. If I allow myself to fall apart over something I can't change or control, I might not recover."

We sit there a few more minutes before she leaves. I go into the bathroom, closing the door, turning on the shower and snatching a towel from the shelf. Placing it to my mouth, I scream into it while sliding down to the floor.

Chapter 3

Standing in front of the floor length mirror in my closet, I turn from side to side admiring the purple jumpsuit I have on. Tonight, there is a dinner party Harvey planned months ago with a small number of our family and friends. A party I asked him not to do and now I'll be the one looking foolish in front of everybody. I stare at my reflection thinking back on this time last year.

"*You look amazing,*" *Harvey says from behind me.*

"*You don't think it's too much. I am almost fifty, you know.*"

"*Babe, you're my sexy forty-nine-year-old, caramel colored lover who is wearing the mess out of these shorts and I can't wait to show you off tonight.*"

"Is that so?" I turn around placing my arms around his neck.

"It is." He kisses me.

"You talked me into this dinner but next year, I want to do something crazy for my birthday."

"Crazy, huh?"

"Yeah, like zip lining over Vegas or skinny dipping in Cancun. I'll be 50 and I want it to be one for the books."

"Then your wish is my command."

"You look beautiful." Haven's voice startles me, and I quickly wipe the tears.

She comes over, intertwining her arm in mine.

"Thank you, baby."

"Are you okay?" she asks.

"No," I smile at her. "Last year, I told your dad I wanted to do something crazy for my birthday. I didn't know it would consist of getting divorce. Funny how you get what you ask for."

"Mom don't do that." She moves in front of me. "You didn't ask for this. Dad is a jackass and he's the only one to blame."

"I have some fault too because I should have noticed something was wrong. I'm a marriage counselor for God's sake. How could I have missed this?"

"You can't miss what wasn't there to see." My sister Denise says from behind me. "Wondah, tonight is about you and I know your foundation has been shaken but you're still standing, and you will get through this."

I let out a long sigh.

"If you want, we can cancel the dinner." Haven says.

"No, I need something to take my mind off your ugly ass daddy. So, let's get through it and I'll deal with everything else tomorrow."

"I love you."

"I love you too."

"Sister, take all the time you need."

When they leave, I look up and close my eyes. "Father, I need your strength."

I take one last look in the mirror before walking down the hall.

Thirty minutes later, I stand at the head of the table, in the backyard which has been decorated for the dinner and look over those in attendance. Haven, my sister Denise and her husband Daniel, my niece Sharda and her husband Chad, my friend Angelique and husband Ethan, Harvey's sister Haley, his cousin Timothy and wife Jayla.

"Thank you all for coming tonight to celebrate my birthday. I know it's weird although nobody has said anything so let me address the elephant in the room. For a gift this year, Harvey gave me divorce papers and none of you can be more shocked, disgusted or hurt than me. I never guessed I'd be turning 50 and getting a divorce from the man I thought I'd spend life on earth with. Anyway," I sigh,

"I can't change things, and neither will I allow it to ruin my birthday. With this being said, don't feel sorry for me. I'll get over this." I raise my glass. "Happy mother-freaking birthday to me!"

*****

3 AM and I'm sitting next to the window in my bedroom looking out at the moon's reflection on the water in the neighborhood lake. After everybody left the dinner, I couldn't fall asleep, so I've been here thinking. Well, questioning.

How could I miss the signs?

How could I not know my husband didn't love me anymore?

What did I do wrong?

What do I do with myself?

Who am I?

For the last 30 years, it's been Harvey and Wondah, Wondah and Harvey. We met in January 1990, when I was twenty-one and he, twenty and hit it off instantly. I don't believe in coincidences or soul mates, however the connection we shared, it had to be God. Every college graduation, the birth of our daughter and the highs and lows of life has been us. Now it's just Wondah. I twirl the wedding ring on my finger before getting up from the chair. I pace at the foot of the bed as tears fall.

"Was it all a lie? Did I imagine the happiness I laid down with last night? Am I losing my mind?"

I lean against the edge of the bed when the light from his closet catches my eye. Opening the door, I go inside to see he's taken only a few of his clothes. I run my hand over the designer suits and shoes lining the wall. I pull out the drawers holding cuff links, watches and ties.

Removing the Rolex, I purchased for our anniversary this year, I turn it over to read the inscription. *Time has proven, the best is yet to be 1.17.93*

"Ha," I scoff throwing the watch into the wall. Once it hits the floor, anger begins to burn my chest causing me to snatch the clothes from their places. "How dare you," I scream. "I gave you all of me. How dare you walk away like I'm nothing. Twenty-nine years and this is what I get in return. You made promises. You're a liar."

"Mom, what are you doing?" Haven asks. "Mom."

I pull away when she grabs my arm.

"Mom, you're scaring me?"

"I'm scaring you, but not your raggedy ass daddy who turned into somebody I don't recognize? That's a joke. You want to know what I'm doing? Getting rid of his ass like he did me." I stomp pass her out of the bedroom and to the utility closet where I grab the box of large garbage bags.

"You don't have to do this," she tells me. "Mom, please stop."

"No," I yell turning back causing her to jump. "He wants to throw me away like trash, let me return the favor. Now move." I order through clenched teeth.

Back in the closet, I fill bag after bag with every piece of clothes Harvey owns. Tired, sweaty and out of breath, I load every free inch of space inside my truck with all it can take.

"Mom," Haven screams. "Mom, where are you going?"

Without shoes, I take my key fob and pull of the driveway, making the twenty-two-minute drive to the nearest thrift store donation box. Standing here after unloading the truck, I wish I had gas and a lighter like Angela Bassett in Waiting to Exhale to burn all this shit up. Instead, I get back into my truck and when I press the ignition button and see the bags, I cry.

Chapter 4

Later in the afternoon, I'm sitting on the patio smoking a rum flavored cigar from Chicks & Cigars, sipping on Harvey's Willet Reserve Bourbon and listening to Tink. I hear the door open, but I don't look up.

"Where are my clothes?" Harvey's voice booms. "Wondah, don't you hear me talking to you? Where are my things?"

I grab my phone and replay the song, "Motives" and begin singing.

"My love was real but I'm questioning yours. I should've known we were falling apart. My intuition was telling me you wasn't shit from the start. Tell me you want me and then leave me lonely."

"Are you done?" he yells.

I stop the music, stand up blowing smoke in his face before putting the cigar out and getting my things. Walking pass him, he grabs my arm and I look him in the eyes.

"Unless you want your face bashed in, I suggest you let me go."

"Are you really being this childish? I came to get some more of my things, only to find you cleared out my closet. What did you do with my clothes?"

"I told you to get your shit."

"I couldn't take everything."

"Sounds like your problem. Dude, get out of my house."

"It's still my house too, until the divorce is final." He states following me inside.

"Not if I burn this motherfucker down."

"Why are you doing this? Can't we be amicable?"

"Amicable?" I laugh. "You filed for divorce behind my back, decided to deliver the papers on my birthday and you want us to be friendly. I think the fuck not and the fact this bottle hasn't met your head and you your demise is me being amicable."

"Just tell me where my stuff is, and I'll leave."

"In the garage."

He rushes out. "There's only two bags out there."

"I know. The rest are at the thrift store. You better be glad I spared the Rolexes." I reply pushing the shoe box until it falls to the floor. "Now get out."

He bends down to pick them up.

"You scratched the faces."

"Whoops," I laugh.

"Which thrift store Wondah?" he questions.

"Figure it out."

The next morning, Haven and I walk into Oak Street Baptist Church. I smile at all the children dressed in their Easter dresses and suits, pausing when I see Harvey talking to one of the deacons near the door.

"Good morning Wondah and happy belated birthday. I pray it was blessed and memorable."

"Good morning Deacon Johnson and thank you. Oh yes, it was definitely memorable. Harvey didn't tell you? I was gifted a divorce."

"What?" he exclaims looking from Harvey to me. Then he laughs. "You're kidding right?"

I turn my head to Harvey who's suddenly mute.

"Nope, apparently my husband has had enough. Which means, we won't be chairing the marriage ministry anymore. Oh, happy Resurrection Sunday."

"Harvey, what in the hell?" I walk off as Deacon Johnson lays into him to find a seat in the middle of the sanctuary. Service starts and the choir sings "Let Me Touch You" by Kirk Franklin. By the time my niece Sharda grabs the microphone, I feel something rising in my spirit I don't like.

"Let me touch You and see if You are real. Even though, I know my heart Your hands can heal, but sometimes I get discouraged and I need Your strength and shield. Jesus. Let me touch You and see if You are real." She sings.

I close my eyes, praying for God to move quickly.

"Please God," I whisper. "I need you."

By the time Pastor Brielle Jordan gets up, I'm trying not to disconnect from the service.

"Good morning mighty oaks." Her voice roars. "This is the day the Lord has made, let us rejoice and be glad in it. It is once again we've joined together to give God praise on a day set aside to remember the sacrifice Jesus made many years ago. Will you go with me to our pointed scripture found in Matthew 27, verses 45 and 46."

She waits until everyone is standing.

"It reads, *"at noon, darkness fell across the whole land until three o'clock. At about three o'clock, Jesus called out with a loud voice, "Eli, Eli, lema sabachthani?" which means "My God, my God, why have you abandoned me?"* For the sake of our note takers, my subject today is when all seems lost. Tell your neighbor, when all seems lost."

I look at Haven. "When all seems lost."

Pastor Brielle continues. "I've experienced some trials and tribulations in my life. Most of them were caused by my selfish desires, premature thinking, foolishness of the flesh and downright stupidity. I've faced times of hardship I didn't think I would make it through. Dark nights I had to tarry with, burdens I had to carry and times I should have died in my sin. Yet, in everything I've faced I could always turn to God, repent and be forgiven. I could pray for a solution by opening the Bible to find a way out of my situation. I could fast and receive and answer. Talk to God and He'd talk back.

When my enemies did me wrong and I wanted to strike back, His words tell me in Romans 12:19, *"Dear friends, never take revenge. Leave that to the righteous anger of God. For the Scriptures say, "I will take revenge; I will pay them back," says the LORD."* When I wanted to be bitter towards folk who stabbed me in the back, Leviticus 19:18 tells me, *"Do not seek revenge or bear a grudge against any of your people but love your neighbor as yourself. I am the LORD."* But then something happens. A storm shows up and it feels like it'll never end. A catastrophe kicks down the door to your heart and you feel you might not survive this. Death leaves and takes with it a piece of your lungs and it feels like you can't breathe.

And all the scriptures can't soothe the ache in your soul because while the Bible gives us hope God will take care of us in whatever situation, what do you do when it feels like it's God you're up against? When it feels like the person you've counted on has abandoned you? What do you do when it seems like you're married to suffering and no divorce lawyer will take the case? What do you do when it seems like you've stepped in quick sand and the more you struggle, the harder it becomes to breathe? For here we are, on another Resurrection Sunday morning—

I bolt from my seat and out of the sanctuary.

Chapter 5

"Are you okay?" Denise asks when I open the stall door.

"Nope, but I have to be." I pause looking at myself in the mirror before washing my hands. "Don't I?"

"No, you don't. Wondah, you're facing something you never have before and it's okay to not be okay. Sister look at me. What you're going through isn't something new upon the face of the earth and neither is it the first storm you've weathered. You'll survive this. However, it doesn't have to be today, this week or month."

"Two days ago, I thought I was happily married, only to find out I was just married. It's crazy because I thought he was my person, like Meredith and Derrick on Grey's Anatomy." I shake my head, wiping the tears. "Here I was, banking on death parting us, all the while he was going through the motions until he got tired of me. What kind of man does this after twenty-seven years of marriage?"

"Men don't do this sis. Immature, small minded, stupid creatures of the male species create pain like what you're going through." She tells me.

I grip the sink. "I have so much anger building in me and I don't like how it's making me feel. I want to hurt that man." I hit the counter. "Now I understand what can make a person snap."

"Let me pray for you."

I shake my head. "I don't need prayer, I need to make him hurt."

She pulls me into her, wrapping her arms around me as my arms fall to the side.

"God, you're the only one who can heal my sister of this hurt and deliver her from the pain and anger permeating through her body. God, you're the only one who can show her this isn't her end nor fault. Father deliver my sister and be there for her. Even when she turns away and closes her ears to you, continue to speak until your voice supersedes everything else. I trust you Father with my sister's life because you trusted me with your spirit. This I pray, amen."

I wrap my arms around her, allowing my tears to fall as my grip tightens because I know if I let go, I may walk away from this church and God.

"God, restore my sister."

Someone walks in. I step back wiping my face.

"Let's go somewhere," she says. "You're on vacation next week and I could use the change of scenery."

I turn to the mirror to fix my face.

"Maybe we should." I agree. "When I get back, I'm going to put the house on the market."

"You love that house."

"I did, but I don't need as much space anymore nor the reminder of what was."

She opens her mouth and I put my hand up. "I need to do this. You may not understand but please support me."

She sighs. "Okay. I'm with you one hundred percent."

Walking back into the sanctuary and taking my seat, Haven touches my leg. I smile to assure her I'm okay, even if I don't believe it.

"Anybody ever been there? Found yourself in the middle of the floor with your arms wrapped tight around you, crying My God, My God, why have you abandoned me." Pastor Brielle asks. "Ever been in your car after trying to be strong but a sob erupts from your belly and you're wondering where is God and why has He deserted you? While standing at the grave of your loved one and although you know to be absent from the body means they are present with the Lord, it doesn't stop your tears or asking, God where are you.

Yes, it may seem like you're all alone. In your pain, exhaustion, anger, confusion and trouble it may feel as though all seems lost; but baby God won't leave you. And somewhere in the midst of what you're facing and surrounded by your enemies, you'll find the strength to have a moment with your Father. This time when you speak to Him, it'll be only for God's understanding.

Why? Well, it's right here in the text. In Matthew 27, when Jesus cried Eli, Eli, lema sabachthani, His enemies around Him couldn't understand Him and thought He was crying out for Elijah. Yet, God was showing His face by confusing the enemies of Jesus.

You know what happens when your enemies are confused? Number one, they'll do things for you they shouldn't. Bible says, immediately one of them ran and took a sponge, filled it with sour wine and put it on a reed, and offered it to Him to drink. They offered wine to a man who is on the verge of death while He's hanging on a cross bleeding, in pain and exhausted because they were confused."

I glance at Harvey who's looking straight ahead. Since Friday morning, he's shown no emotion towards me. It's almost like we're strangers and haven't shared the last thirty years of our life together. My leg begins to shake, and my hand rubs up and down my leg.

I close my eyes, taking a deep breath. Haven nudges me.

"Can we go?" I ask her.

She nods. Walking to the car, it feels like I'm moving outside of my body.

"Mom, slow down. What's wrong?"

"How can he act like everything we've gone through never existed? He's sitting at the front of the church like he's a good Christian man when he isn't. No God-fearing man hurts people like this."

I abruptly stop when I see his car.

"Mom, no." Haven grabs me. "No, don't do this. I know you're hurt, but I will not allow you to embarrass yourself."

"I'm already embarrassed." I angrily reply.

She takes my hand, pulling me to the truck.

"Get in," she orders before slamming the door after me.

"I'm sorry and thank you," I say ending the silence once we've left the parking lot.

"You don't have to apologize, but you will have to find a better way to get through this. Self-destruction isn't the answer."

I lay my head back. "I know."

Chapter 6

Haven has gone back to California where she's currently working at the Walt Disney Company in their animation department. Me, it's 1:19 AM and I'm up. In fact, I haven't been able to sleep the past five days since everything happened. Denise and I didn't go out of town because I changed my mind. Getting away sounded good, but I'm not in the mood to be anyone's company.

I was served with the actual divorce summons on Friday. This Negro had me served at our house at 6 AM in the morning by a sheriff's deputy. As if things aren't embarrassing enough. Later that afternoon, I met with my attorney, Nina, to fill out all of the appropriate documents necessary for this mess to be over as quickly as possible. She explained everything and said it's going to take sixty days from the date of filing before a court date will be set for the final divorce hearing, seeing it's an uncontested divorce. He technically filed on April 1st and I guess the April Fool's joke was on me.

I take my journal, drawing over the date I wrote.

June 1, 2020

June first will be sixty days. Sixty days is how long I have to wait to be free from a man who woke up one day no longer loving who I am. He no longer desired the life we built or maybe he no longer desired me. Sixty days. Sixty days is all it takes to dissolve what thirty years created.

Shaking the thoughts away, I close the journal and pick up my phone to scroll Facebook. Clicking on Harvey's page, I realize he's unfriended me. "Bastard," I mumble going through the few things I can see. I lay the phone down and slide under the cover. Turning on my side, I glare at the pillow that used to belong to him. Picking it up and pressing it to my nose, it still smells like him. Getting angry, I throw the covers back and begin snatching everything from the bed. Pillows, sheets, comforter … everything. As I pull, I scream. Throwing it all into the middle of the floor, I rush into the kitchen getting the largest knife from the drawer. Getting back into the bedroom, I start to cut up the mattress.

"You low down, dirty, piece of shit. I've slept next to you never knowing you'd grown tired of me. In this bed." I stab more spaces. "In this bed is where you held me knowing what you were planning to do. In this bed." I scream continuing to force the knife in and out. "In this bed is where we made plans. It's where you made me promises. In this bed. You motherfucker."

I stab the knife one final time, leaving it there before knocking everything off his nightstand. I bend down, picking up his reading glasses and breaking them in two. The last book he was reading, I tear out the pages. The picture of us, I sling it into the wall.

"You walk away after inflicting this much pain." I fall into the pile of covers on the floor. "How could he do this?"

The next morning, I'm awaken by Isabel, our housekeeper.

"Ay Dios mio." She exclaims. "Oh Mrs. Wondah." She says with sadness in her voice kneeling beside me. "What's wrong? Did something happen to Mr. Harvey?"

"He's gone. Harvey is gone." I bury my face into the covers and cry.

She sucks in air. "Lo siento mi amiga. Lo siento mucho. Que su alma descanse en paz."

"He's not dead." I correct when she says may his soul rest in peace. "He left me."

"Tonta, Mrs. Wondah. That man is a fool."

"I agree." I tell her sitting up. "Thank you, Isabel, but you don't have to stay today. I'm going to clean this mess up myself."

"Mrs. Wondah, you don't have to do everything by yourself. Let me help you."

"I don't even know what I need." I admit.

She rubs my cheek. "How about you start with a shower and I'll start the coffee."

Forty-five minutes later, I walk into the kitchen to coffee, toast and eggs.

"You didn't have to cook breakfast. I don't have much of an appetite."

"You need to eat. Sit." She demands.

I smile at her. Isabel is a sixty-two-year-old, head strong woman. She's been with us for over twenty years after becoming Haven's nanny when she was two and never left. Now, she comes two times per week and I think it's because we both enjoy each other's company.

"I can have Tony move the mattress for you." She says referring to her son.

"He can take the entire bed, the nightstands and have him throw out the bedding too."

"Are you sure?"

"Yes. It's time for something new."

She pats my hand.

Later on, I stop by Ashley Home Store to purchase a new bedroom set. I choose a dark blue tufted bed with some decorative metallic side tables and matching dresser. They can't deliver them until Wednesday which is fine. It'll give me time to clear the room and maybe paint.

Getting into the car, my sister Denise calls.

"Hey." I answer.

"Hey. I'm calling to check on you."

"That's sweet of you, but I'm fine."

"You don't have to lie to me. What are you up too?" she questions.

"Just leaving Ashley's getting some new bedroom furniture. Speaking of which, do you think Daniel can send someone by to repaint my master?"

"Sister, slow down. Are you sure this is what you want to do? Have you even spoken to Harvey?"

"Speak to him for what? You don't honestly think this is something we can work through, do you?"

"Why not? You all have been together thirty years Wondah. There has to be something."

"Something, huh?" I chuckle. "Something like what sis? You think time forgives what he did? This funky face dog handed me papers of divorce on my birthday without ever mentioning wanting out. If there was something, it should have prevented that. So, please spare me. We will never come back from this and neither are there words in the English, Spanish, French, Caribbean, Nigerian or whatever other language he could speak to make me forgive him. Fuck him. Can Daniel help me or not?"

"I'll have him call you."

"Thank you."

I release the call and throw the phone into the passenger seat.

"Ugh." I scream out.

Chapter 7

Two nights later, I'm laying on the couch flipping through TV channels. Settling on an episode of Married with Children, I drop the remote. Staring at the TV, I haven't heard a word of what's being said because my eyes keep drifting to the family photos on the mantle.

I sit up. In a huff, I go into the kitchen where I down two shots of Hennessy, straight.

"He walks away like I meant nothing."

Another shot.

"I've been with you since I was twenty-one years old and you promised me forever."

Another shot.

"I guess it's fuck Wondah, huh."

Another shot.

"After everything." I yell. "You said we'd retire together and travel the world."

Another shot.

"Why did you lie to me?"

Another shot.

Walking into the living room holding the bottle and pressing another shot to my lips, my eyes land on the picture we took at our anniversary dinner in January.

"Okay, one more shot. Do something that shows you love each other." The photographer requests, and Harvey pulls me into him, kissing all over my face.

He comes over and shows us the picture.

"We're definitely keeping this one."

Swallowing the liquid, I throw the glass into it. Going over, I swipe all the remaining pictures onto the floor. Turning, I see his recliner. Sitting the bottle on the table, I rush into the kitchen for a knife. Returning, I begin to stab the chair, over and over.

Tired and sweaty, I step back wincing from pain I feel in the bottom of my foot. "Got damn it," I yell hopping over to the couch. "Your raggedy ass is still causing pain." I get the bottle and fall back taking another swig of the alcohol. "Serves me right though because I should have seen this coming. I'm Wondah freaking Jennings, marriage counselor extraordinaire." I laugh drinking more. "I help people save their marriage and I couldn't even see mine was failing. Talk about the irony in that. Okay God, cheers," I lift the bottle before swallowing a little more, "you got me with this one."

"Mrs. Wondah, please wake up. Mrs. Wondah."

I push the hands away touching me. "Stop."

"Gracias Dios. She's waking up. Mrs. Wondah, can you hear me?"

"Stop yelling," I order opening my eyes to see Isabel.

"Ma'am, hi, hello. Can you hear me?"

I turn my head to see a strange guy in my face.

"Who the hell are you?"

"My name is Carlton, an EMT. You have a pretty bad cut on your foot and Isabel was having trouble waking you. Do you know where you are?"

I sit up and my head spins.

"Whoa." I laugh. "It must have been some party."

"Ma'am, please don't move. Your foot is going to need stitches and you've lost a good bit of blood. Not enough to need a transfusion or anything, but I suggest allowing us to transport you to Methodist University."

"No, I'm fine."

"Mrs. Wondah, you're not fine," Isabel protests. "Here, drink this."

I swat her away as Denise rushes in, stopping and covering her mouth. "Oh my God."

"Aw hell. Calm down, it's worse than it looks." I tell her.

"Sir, how bad is it?" she asks the EMT, ignoring me.

"She's going to need stitches in her foot and possibly some fluids." Carlton replies to her.

"I'm not going to the hospital. Get out of my house and leave me alone." I demand.

"I'll take care of it," Denise assures him. "I'm a doctor and will ensure she gets seen."

After they leave Denise stands in front of me with her arms folded. "What were you thinking? You could have bled to death. God, thank you for looking after the foolish."

"Girl, you're being dramatic. It's a small cut, chill." I stand but instantly fall back yelping in pain.

"Still think it's only a small cut? Come on and let me take you to the ER."

"I'm fine."

"You're not fine." She yells. "There's glass everywhere and I don't even want to know how much of this," she holds the bottle up, "you drank. Now, stop being stubborn and let's go. Isabel, thank you for calling me."

"You're welcome and Mrs. Wondah, I'll get everything cleaned up for you."

Chapter 8

"How are you feeling?" Denise asks walking into the exam room where I've been for over three hours.

I stare at the wall.

"Sis, talk to me."

"Can you take me home?" I question.

"Don't shut me out. Not now."

"I'm tired and not in the mood for talking. Thank you for taking care of me and I'm sorry for worrying you."

"Fine. We will talk about this later."

After getting home and struggling with the crutches, I'm chained to for at least three weeks, I finally get to the couch.

"Here." Denise hands me her phone. I sigh when I see Haven's name.

"I'll call her back."

She puts it on speaker. "Go ahead Haven."

"Mom, are you okay?"

"Peachy."

"This is serious," she yells. "Do you know how scared I was when Isabel called to say she couldn't wake you and there was blood everywhere?"

"Isabel shouldn't have called you."

"What else was she supposed to do? She thought you were dead."

I sigh. "I'm fine, it's only a cut."

"A cut requiring eight stitches in the bottom of your foot." Denise adds. "I won't even say anything about the alcohol which increases your chances of bleeding."

"You just did." I scoff.

"Had Isabel not found you—

"Enough," I yell. "I made a mistake. Yes, I could have bled to death, but I didn't. I shouldn't have been drinking, but I was. I get it. I didn't use sound judgment and I'm sorry. I apologize for scaring the both of you and Denise I appreciate you taking care of me, but I'm not a child so stop scolding me like I am."

"Auntie, I'm going to let you deal with her because I can't. Mom, I love you and when you need me, call."

"Wondah, we're worried about you." Denise says after putting the phone in her pocket.

"It was a mistake." I hiss. "It's not like I tried to commit suicide. I stepped on a piece of freaking glass and you're acting like I slit my wrists."

"No, I'm acting like someone who is witnessing her big sister go through a storm that has destroyed what she's known about her life and left her angry."

"Yeah, well she can handle herself." I mock.

"Wondah, I know what the effects of anger does to a person and so do you. Unresolved emotions can destroy you and everything in its path. Sister, you don't have to be strong for me because I won't judge your weak moments. Talk to me."

"And say what? Huh? How do you expect me to put what I'm feeling into words when I can't? I'm mad as hell and at this moment, talking can't soothe that. My husband of twenty-seven years had divorce papers drawn up behind my back. The smug motherfucker didn't even fight, hell I didn't even know there was something to fight about, he just walked away like this was a drunken marriage in Vegas he annulled. Do you know how it feels?"

She doesn't say anything.

"I didn't think so. You still have a husband, but when I roll over at night, all I see is the empty bed where he used to sleep with his leg over mine. Your husband still comes home, mine destroyed his. So, excuse me for not acting like myself."

"You're right and I won't apologize for my husband still being here because he and Harvey are not the same. Harvey is a jackass who broke your heart, but he doesn't deserve the power you're giving him to break you."

"He's not breaking me." I refute.

"He is and drinking until you pass out isn't going to help."

"You act like I'm an alcoholic. I was at home and decided to take a few shots hoping it would numb me because I'm hurting."

"Numbing isn't a fix for the problem."

"I wasn't trying to fix a problem. I didn't even know a problem existed until a week ago." I yell. "I drank because I'm freaking hurting and it's far better to drink and destroy the material things rather than kill him because that's really what I want."

She glares at me.

"Don't I deserve space and time to be angry?" I ask.

"You definitely do, but sis, in a few hours the medicine I used to numb your foot will wear off. When it does, you're going to experience pain from glass piercing your foot. You want to know why? The medicine is only temporary, the same with alcohol. It may numb you momentarily, yet the only way to stop the pain is to heal."

"Yeah, well consider this part of my healing. Again, thank you for taking care of me, but you can go."

She comes over, throwing her arms around me. "I love you and I have to believe you'll get through this because you're my big sister who can handle anything. I'll be back with dinner."

When she leaves, I fall back onto the couch.

You're my big sister who can handle anything.

"What if I can't this time?" I cry. "What if I can't handle this?"

Chapter 9

The following Monday, I struggle to get out the backseat of the Uber with the crutches. Fumbling with the door, I finally get inside. Asha sees me and rushes over taking my bag.

"Wondah, oh my God, what happened to you? Wait, don't tell me you got hurt doing some nasty stuff with Harvey while you were on vacation." She laughs.

"Harvey asked for a divorce."

She pauses then laughs. "Stop playing."

I look at her.

"You're serious?"

"Yep."

"I don't understand." She says with a look of sadness.

"Neither do I, yet it is what it is."

She follows me into my office.

"I, uh, I'm at a loss for words." She stops. "If you and Harvey can't make it, I know for sure marriage isn't for me."

"No, don't do that." I say to her. "Never set goals for your life based on someone else. Yes, I'm hurt my marriage is over, yet I still believe in the joining together of two people and the sanctity of marriage. Why do you think I showed up today? Although my heart was shattered by the one man I thought never would, I'm here ready to help couples repair what's broken in theirs because marriage didn't fail me, Asha, Harvey did."

"Wow." She says wiping tears from her face and coming over to give me a hug. "Your strength encourages me. Thank you. I'll get out of here and let you prepare for the day. Your first appointment is in an hour. Ping me if you need anything."

Once the door closes, I sit in my chair putting my head in my hands. "God, only you can help me through this. Please don't allow my flesh to speak in areas my spirit shall do the talking. Fill me with your wisdom and guide me to help those who will sit before us in this place. My flesh may be weak, but my spirit is willing and as long as you let the Holy Spirit dwell within me, I'll do what you've called me to do. Help me to help your people. In the name of Jesus, I pray, amen."

I stand and balance myself before grabbing the jar of Holy oil and making my way over to the area where I counsel couples, praying for God's presence to fill the room. Once I'm done, I take my iPad and Apple pencil, placing it on the table beside the chair. Sitting back at my desk, I turn on my laptop when my phone dings with a notification. I pick it up and see a text from Denise.

My Sister Denise: "Rejoice in hope, be patient in tribulation, be constant in prayer." – Romans 12:12. I love you sister and I pray you have a great day.

Me: I love you too and pray the same for you.

An hour later, I'm watching the banter of a young couple who had a premarital consultation with me a few weeks ago I use as a session to learn about them as individuals. Since they've decided to continue counselling, today begins their sessions together.

"I'm sorry," Gabby says touching the hand of her fiancé Drake.

"It's okay," I assure her. "Are you both ready to begin?"

They nod.

"Great. Why are you getting married?"

"I love him," she beams.

"And I love her."

"Is this the only reason?" I question.

"Of course not," she says. "Doctor Jennings, I've known since I was a little girl marriage is what I desire. I've dreamed of how it'll be walking down the aisle to my prince charming and us starting our lives. Marriage has always been my goal and I'm choosing to marry Drake because I can see myself sharing a lifetime with him. We both come from homes that have shown us healthy examples of marriage and it's what we want."

"Drake is this how you feel?"

"Yes ma'am." He sits up. "Like Gabby said, my mom and dad have shown me evidence marriage can work, and I believe in it. I also trust God and if this union between us wasn't meant, He wouldn't allow it. I'm getting married because I love Gabby and I want to share the rest of my life with her."

They smile at each other.

"Gabby, what is your definition of a husband and what do you expect from Drake?"

"A husband is a provider, protector and the head of his house. He's the one who God has put as my covering. I expect him to love me like God loves the church, protect me, provide for me and be someone I can submit too. When we marry, we'll become one flesh and I expect him to love and treat me like he does himself."

"Drake, how do you feel about Gabby's response?"

"I'm in agreement with it because as the man, it is my responsibility. I've seen my dad be the head of his house for over thirty years, so I know how to be a great husband."

"You know what your dad has allowed you to see and no offense, but you aren't your dad and Gabby is not his wife. You have to become the husband that fits your house. Sure, you can learn from the ways of your dad, however what works for your parent's house may not work for yours and you have to learn the difference."

"Why?" he questions with a confused look.

"If you go into your marriage shaping it like your parent's or even Gabby's parents, you run the risk of failing each other because you'll be building on a foundation neither of you created. Let's say, for example, your dad brings his wife, your mom, flowers every Thursday and she enjoys it. You and

Gabby marry, and you carry that tradition into your home, but she isn't fond of flowers. Instead of telling you, she allows you to do it because it's what you think a husband is supposed to do even though she doesn't like it. Ten years pass and one day she finally admits it. Are you justified in being angry at her for not saying anything or is she right for accepting and keeping her mouth closed?"

"We'd both be wrong. Me for assuming and her for accepting."

"I don't like flowers." She admits, and they laugh.

"My point is, you can take direction from your parents to start the plans, but the building should be up to the two of you."

"Makes sense," he says.

"Drake, what is your definition of a wife and what do you expect from Gabby?"

"A wife is a helpmate, a good thing from the Lord, a crown for me, builder of our home and the carrier of my seed. I expect her to love, honor, respect and trust me. I don't want her to bow down to me, but I want her to let me lead as the man of the house. I also don't expect her to withhold herself from me sexually."

"Gabby, how do you feel about this?"

"The only thing we're not in agreement on is the sexual part of our relationship. I get what he means by not withholding myself, but there may be times I say not tonight, and I need him to be okay with it."

"Drake, are you okay with that?"

"Yeah, as long as it's not every night. Doc, I'm a man who has needs and she's the only woman I plan to spend the rest of my life with. If I can't get what I desire from her, what else am I supposed to do."

"I understand, and I'll never intentionally push you into the bed of someone else but don't make me feel bad for not wanting to be pounded twice a day, seven days a week. Three to four times a week, I can do, but not every day. Women need time for our bodies to recover."

"Deal." Drake says.

She rubs his hand.

"Let's switch gears for a moment. I know each of you were raised in strong biblical families. Outside of prayer, how do you plan to deal with conflict that may arise when we live in a natural world where evil roams to destroy marriages?"

"We'll do like we've always done. Along with prayer, we'll fast, talk and figure out a resolution satisfying each of us."

"Drake, sometimes the resolution won't satisfy the both of you. It's like deciding on dinner. You have a taste for Chinese and she wants seafood."

"But I'd be okay with letting him choose Chinese." Gabby cuts in.

"Marriage isn't about letting him choose, it's being inwardly and wholeheartedly okay with his choice. See, it's one thing to let him pick and it's another to resent him for it later."

"We won't have those problems." She states. "Doctor Jennings, do you believe in God?"

"Of course." I reply.

"Then why would you say outside of prayer? Don't you know God is all you need?"

"Gabby, if God is all you need, why get married?"

Her mouth opens and closes.

"As believers, followers and children of God, He is who we need but not all we need."

"Philippians four and nineteen says, "But my God shall supply all your needs according to His riches in glory by Christ Jesus."" She tells me.

"When Paul told the Philippians this, it was after they'd surrendered their finances and material possessions to God's service. He was letting them know in response to their actions, God would supply all they need. Need meaning sustenance or whatever they needed for the journey. For us, God supplies our need through His glory of oxygen, food, water, clothes, family, friends and etc. In the same way, He also supplies us with things when coupled with prayer and faith, helps us to survive this world."

They are both staring intently.

"Hear me clearly. I didn't ask you that question to second guess the power and ability of God, I did for you to understand you'll need help. Yes, prayer is great but so is coping mechanisms, conflict resolutions, trust, the ability to budget and maintain finances, a plan of how to raise children, how often you'll be intimate, making decisions together, dealing with the warfare of this world among many other things. Do you both grasp what I'm saying?"

"In other words, it takes work." Drake answers.

"No, it takes a lot of work, yet it's worth every drop of sweat and tears. What I need you to understand, you're going to need prayer and actions. Now, before your next session, I want each of you to write out where you see your marriage in five years pertaining to faith, family and finance.

Complete it separately without revealing it to the other and we'll discuss it together."

"Thank you, Doctor Jennings."

"You're welcome and I'll see you next week."

Chapter 10

Getting home, I kick off my shoe, drop my bag on the table before removing my phone and sliding it in my shirt. Exhaling, I balance the crutches.

"Good evening Mrs. Wondah."

I jump at the sound of Isabel's voice.

"God, you scared me. I wasn't expecting you to be here."

"I apologize." She says looking down at the floor.

"Isabel, is everything alright?"

"There's something I need to talk to you about."

"Okay."

"Mr. Harvey contacted me this morning asking if I'd be willing to work for him part time."

"Isabel, you don't need my permission for that."

"I know, but my loyalty is to you." She tells me.

"I appreciate you, however there are no sides to take and choosing to work for him doesn't void the relationship you and I have. You've been a part of our family for over twenty years, so it makes you family and it won't change now Harvey and I are getting a divorce"

She hugs me. "Thank you, Mrs. Wondah. I left you some of my Abuela's famous paella in the refrigerator. She also told me to give you this."

"What is it?"

"It's an herbal salve for your foot. She says it'll help you heal faster."

"Will it work on my heart too?"

She touches my hand.

"Tell your Abuela, I said gracias."

"I will, and I'll be here Wednesday for your furniture to be delivered."

"Thanks, because I'm sick of that guest room."

Once she leaves, I lean against the counter taking deep breaths. Pushing away, I go over to the refrigerator and pull out the container. Popping it into the microwave, I press the button for three minutes before getting the bottle of wine. I sit it on the counter, grab a fork and wait. After the microwave dings, I get the bowl and sit. Exhaling, I put the wine bottle to my lips and gulp. Looking down at the food, I slide a forkful in and swallow, repeating it twice then replacing the top.

I stand, putting the wine bottle into the front of my pants and picking up the salve. After arming the alarm and turning off the lights, I make my way to the bedroom. Flopping on the side of the bed to catch my breath, I sit the bottle on the nightstand dreading the time it's going to take me to shower.

"May as well get it over with." I tell myself.

After an hour-long struggle with showering, dressing and bandaging my foot; I'm now in the middle of the bed scrolling Facebook. Against my better judgment, I click on Harvey's page. Forgetting I'm no longer his friend, I log out and into the fake profile I created. I smile when I see he's accepted *Parker's* friend request.

Thumbing down his timeline, he's never posted a lot on his page until now.

His latest post is a picture of a beach with the caption … *Looking forward to a nice getaway this weekend.*

I heart it and reply … *Nothing like the feel of sand in places it doesn't belong to put your mind at ease. Have fun.*

I roll my eyes when a call comes through from a number, I'm not familiar with. I answer and press the speaker.

"This is Wondah."

"Wondah, it's Harvey. Please don't hang up. Hello, are you there?"

"What do you want?"

"In order to remove my name from the accounts at the bank, you have to be there. I know it's short notice, but can you meet me in the morning at 9 AM at the branch near our, I mean your house."

"I thought it couldn't be done until the divorce."

"My attorney said it's fine since you're not contesting it."

"Fine."

"Thank—

I hang up before he can finish and block this number too.

"Raggedy, shrimp face bastard." I throw the phone on the nightstand and grab the bottle of wine. "I know it's short notice." I mock. "It's not like you give a damn about my time or feelings anyway. I hope sand flies eat your ass up while you're sitting on the beach this weekend. Funky goat." I reach into the nightstand and get an Advil PM, swallowing it with more wine.

The next morning, I open my eyes to the sun piercing through the curtains. It reminds me to order black out drapes for the master bedroom from Bed, Bath & Beyond. Harvey never liked them.

"Well, he ain't here no mo." I say out loud.

Touching my watch on the nightstand, I see it's 8:17 AM.

"Oops, looks like I'm going to be late."

I lay there a few more minutes before sitting up and closing my eyes for prayer.

"God, do your thang today. Amen."

Finally leaving the house, the Uber drops me off at the bank at 9:22 AM.

"Good morning ma'am, how may I help you?"

"I need to have my husband's name removed from some accounts."

"Is your husband with you?" she inquires.

"Nope, he's dead."

"I'm sorry for your loss."

I hear someone clear their throat behind me.

"Ma'am, I'm not dead. I'm Harvey Jennings."

I shrug, "He's dead to me so can we get this over with."

"Uh, right this way." She says looking from him to me.

"What do you need from me to hurry this along?" I ask once we're seated.

"Your identification, account number and account passcode."

I hand her my license, bank card and speak the code.

"Are you wanting to close these accounts and start new ones?"

"I'd rather not unless it's my only option because I don't want the hassle of changing everything over."

"It's not necessary, but it's usually the way couples decide to handle things." She states.

"I'm okay with her keeping the old accounts, I only need my name removed and I'll sign whatever documents to relinquish my rights." Harvey adds.

"Isn't that nice of you."

"Mr. Jennings, will you be needing new accounts?" she questions.

"No, I've already taken care of that."

"Dang, you sure don't waste time, do you?" I mockingly say.

The lady looks between the two of us. "Very well. I'll also need your identification. Great, I'll be right back."

"Wondah, what happened to your foot? Are you okay?"

"I got drunk, broke every picture in the living room that contained your ugly ass face and stepped on some glass." I smile. "Yes, I'm great. How are you?"

"I—

"I don't care, truly." I cut him off.

He sighs.

"I'm sorry for hurting you."

"And I'm sorry you're breathing."

"Okay, here's your information back and Mr. Jennings, I'll need you to sign, date and place your fingerprint on this document stating you are giving up your rights to any funds within the checking and savings account which currently has your name."

He signs the papers as she sits behind the desk and begins typing on the computer. Minutes pass and she finally looks up, pulling papers from the printer.

"Mrs. Jennings, here's the copy of your accounts with the removal of Mr. Harvey Jennings. Mr. Jennings, your bank card attached to these accounts are now invalid. Will there be a need for new checks?"

"Nope, I don't use them. Are we done?" I ask.

"Yes ma'am."

I take out my phone and open the Uber app.

"Thank you for banking with Regions, have a great day."

I smile, put my bag across me and stand with the crutches. A gentleman holds the door as I step out of the bank. A few seconds later Harvey walks behind me.

"Wondah," he catches up coming around in front to stop me.

I'm looking at my phone checking the Uber's arrival time.

"Why are you in my face?"

"Will you please give me a moment? There's something I need to tell you." He pauses, and I look over his shoulder to see the door to his car opening. A girl gets out.

"I need to use the restroom." She states before he turns, and she notices me. "Oh."

I look down at her pregnant belly.

"Anette, get back in the car." He orders.

"No, it's time you tell her the truth." She barks at him. "I'm tired of not being able to share my happiness with the world."

He glances at me.

"Tell me what?"

"I'm Harvey's fiancé and we're expecting a baby in four months." She answers.

"Damn, does she pee for you too?" I ask him.

"Wondah, what she said is true, but this isn't the way I wanted you to find out."

"Right," I drag out. "This isn't the way, yet you bring her with you to meet me. So, tell me husband, how did you want me to find out you've been cheating with a girl who looks younger than our daughter and is pregnant."

"Technically, he wasn't meeting you." She gripes.

"Girl don't interrupt grown folks when they're talking because it's the easiest way to get the shit slapped out of you."

"I'm not a girl, old lady. I'm twenty-five."

"Twenty-five," I gasp. "You couldn't find anybody your own age, pervert?"

"Anette get back in the car, please. Wondah, wait. Let me explain."

"No need, my ride is here." I say stepping down next to his car. Balancing myself, I lay one crutch on the side of the car next to his, bringing the other one up and commencing to beating his hood and windshield.

"Twenty-seven years and this is what you do?" I continually inflict the pain onto his car wishing it was him instead. When he tries to grab the crutch, it connects with his side and we both fall into the car. He yelps in pain.

"I'm calling the police," the girl hollers.

"Don't," Harvey groans towards her while he's bent over, clutching his side. "Wondah, please."

"Fuck you," I scream knocking out the side window before repositioning my bag, straightening my clothes, grabbing the other crutch and walking to the Uber. "Hi, are you Pam?"

"Uh, yeah." She stutters.

"Great, I'm Wondah." I reply getting into her car and throwing a finger sign at Harvey and his fiancé.

Chapter 11

On the ride to the office, I use the Allstate app to remove Harvey and his car from the insurance. Sitting back in my chair, I'm thankful Tuesday's are my free days to update charts. Asha doesn't come in unless it's an emergency, so I have the place to myself. I fetch the bottle of bourbon from the desk drawer as my phone rings with a call from Haven. I ignore it. She calls the office. I ignore it. She sends a text.

My Haven: MOM!!!!

I turn the phone face down and pour a drink. If I could pace, that's what I'd be doing.

"Ah," I yell. "Why is this happening to me? I know I haven't always been good and neither have I done everything right but come on God. Is this what I deserve? I dedicated myself to this man, a man you sent by the way and this is what I get in return. I gave him all of me for twenty-nine years and a piece of paper ends it in minutes."

I push away from the desk and when I rise, I trip over my bag and hit the corner of the desk.

Opening my eyes, I jump when I see a man sitting across from me. I look around realizing I'm still in my office.

"Don't be afraid Wondah. God has heard your prayer." He states.

I scoff. "Are you serious? God has heard my prayer? Which one? You know what, don't answer because I don't care anymore. What kind of God would allow His children to suffer like this?"

"Who are you that you cannot suffer? Are you greater than a woman suffering through cancer or a man who's had to watch his wife perish?"

I sit back and look at him.

"Wondah, why do you blame God for your husband leaving? Can He control the actions of a man?"

"He made him, didn't He?"

"He made you too and could He control your actions today?" he rebuts.

"I don't have to listen to this. Get out of my office."

"Who are you to question God's authority on what you deserve?" his voice booms. "Are you not worthy of a little pain?"

"I said get out." I stand and point to the door. "You will not talk to me like this."

"But isn't this the way you speak to God? If you're bold enough to call Him out, then brace yourself while He replies."

"Oh, so now you're God?" I chuckle.

"No, but I stand in God's presence."

"Then stand on the outside of the door because this conversation is over."

He walks closer to me.

"Wondah, God hasn't left you, but have you stopped to think maybe it was you who abandoned Him?"

"You can't be serious right now? I was faithful to my husband, daughter and church. I pay tithes, give offerings, help those who need it, pray and fast."

"Yeah, but where's God?"

"Are you saying God allowed my husband to get another girl pregnant, walk out and treat me like the scum on the bottom of His shoe to teach me a lesson?"

"God didn't allow Harvey to do any of those things, his flesh did. However, do you really think God would stop the thing or person who's hurting His children from leaving?"

"Oh, this was for my good?"

"Don't you think so?" he inquires.

"I'm done with this conversation."

"Wondah, you counsel couples every day and yet, you can't be counseled."

"Maybe I'm not ready to be counseled. Now get out," I scream. "Get out and leave me alone."

He touches me, and my eyes fly open. I groan grabbing my head. Sitting up, I press my back to the side of the desk. Looking at my watch, it's after six in the afternoon. "Was I dreaming?"

The office phone rings and it scares me. I roll to my knees and get up. By the time I plop into the chair, the ringing has stopped. Picking up my cell phone, I see numerous missed calls and texts from Denise and Haven. I press the speaker button when my desk phone rings again.

"This is Wondah."

"I'm kicking your ass." Denise yells. "Why are you ignoring us? We've been calling you for hours."

"I wasn't, well not intentionally. I tripped over my bag and I think I blacked out."

"You what? Where are you?"

"Duh, the office but I'm fine. If you were so worried, why didn't you come looking for me?"

"Trick, I know you're not trying to guilt me. I'm not the one who went all Rambo on your husband's car then goes MIA for hours. Your daughter is at the airport, right now, waiting on a flight to come home because she's worried about you."

I text Haven.

Me: Please don't come home.

Me: I'm sorry for scaring you, it was not my intention but I'm fine.

My Haven: WTF mom!!!

Me: I'm sorry.

She Facetimes me. When it connects, her eyes are red and swollen.

"Haven, I'm so sorry."

"Are you okay?" she sobs. "You're bleeding."

"No." I sigh as tears fall. I hear Denise let out an exasperated breath. "Denise, I'll call you back."

"You won't because I'm headed to get you." She says releasing the call.

"Mom, I get you're angry and you have every right to be, but what is going on? This isn't the woman I've known all my life. The woman I watched from a little girl is strong-willed and stubborn."

"Haven, I'm not perfect and neither am I a bionic woman who can endure everything without flinching. Yes, I'm angry and that anger led me to destroy your father's car. I won't apologize, because the mother," I take a breath. "He deserved it. Did you know he's having a baby with a girl who's not much older than you?"

She looks away and sighs. "I found out last night."

Tears rush from my eyes.

"I wanted to tell you." She whispers, and my sob gets louder.

"What a friend we have in Jesus. All our sins and griefs to bear. What a privilege to carry, everything to God in prayer. Oh, what peace we often forfeit.

Oh, what needless pain we bear. All because we do not carry, everything to God in prayer." Haven sings.

I look at the phone and smile. "I'm so glad you're smart because you suck at singing."

We both laugh. "You needed a reminder that you don't have to carry all of this by yourself. If you aren't ready to talk to your family, at least talk to God."

"God and I are beefing at the moment."

"No, you're beefing with Him, mother."

"Same thang. Haven, thank you and I apologize for scaring you, but you don't need to come home."

"I'm coming because you need me."

"You're right, I do need you however, I also need time to grieve through this loss on my own." I tell her.

"I get it, but not like this. What if dad would have filed charges?"

"I would have beat his ass."

"Mom," she groans.

"Just kidding."

After a few seconds of silence. "Mom?"

I look at the phone.

"You should see dad's car," she laughs. "And you cracked two of his ribs."

"Serves him right."

"You can't do that anymore." She says in between giggles. "Seriously, will you promise to find healthier choices to relieve your anger?"

"I promise."

"I need to cancel this flight. Call me before you go to bed and let's pray together."

"Okay. I love you."

"I love you too."

When the phone goes dark, I scream gripping the desk. With the anger and hurt inside of me, I feel strong enough to turn the whole thing over. "God, how could I have been so stupid."

"You weren't stupid sister."

I jump at the sound of Denise's voice.

"Yes, I was. I didn't know my own husband was cheating. Nise, that girl is six months pregnant and she stood in my face gloating while I felt like the biggest fool."

She rushes over to me. "Wondah, stop this. Stop taking the blame for believing in the stability of your marriage and home. You had no reason to think Harvey would do this. Hell, none of us did. He was great at pretending, apparently."

"I feel like I don't even know who he is anymore. I've been with this man more years than I spent with mom and dad and with him handing me divorce papers, he caused pain in crevices I didn't even know pain could reside. And I'm mad. I'm so mad."

She wraps her arm around me, I lay my head on her stomach and cry.

"You have every right to be because I can't even begin to think what I'd do in your situation. Which is why I'm not holding any of this against you." She smiles. "Now, come on and let's get this head checked out."

After an MRI to rule out a concussion, two stitches on the forehead and a lecture from Denise, I finally make it home. Dropping my bags on the counter in the kitchen, I shower and put on a lounging dress. Going into the kitchen, I deposit the empty wine bottle into the recycle bin before getting another bottle from the bar. Deciding on popcorn for dinner, I place it into the microwave while trying to figure out how to get the wine into the living room without breaking it.

Looking around the kitchen, I get an apron out the drawer and tie it around the right crutch. Sliding the bottle into the front pocket, I make sure it's snug enough.

"Perfect." I say as the microwave dings. Getting two Tylenol from the cabinet, I slide them into the pocket before taking the popcorn, steadying the crutches and making my way into the living room, turning on the movie Dream Girls.

"Yeah, well it's between you too now lil sister," I mimic with the movie. "Tell'em Effie," I scream at the TV. "They can't treat you like that and get away with it." I throw popcorn at the screen. I turn the volume up when she begins to sing and start to belt out the lyrics.

"And I am telling you I'm not going. Even though the rough times are showing, there's just no way, there's no way. We're part of the same place. We're part of the same time. We both share the same blood. We both have the same mind and time and time, we've had so much to see and no, no, no, no, no, no way. I'm not waking up tomorrow morning and finding that there's nobody there."

I sit up on the couch, using the bottle as a microphone. "And I am telling you I'm not going. You're the best man I'll ever know. There's no way I could ever, ever go. No, no, no, no way. No, no, no, no way I'm living without you. Oh, I'm not living without you, not living without you. I don't wanna be free. I'm staying, I'm staying and you, and you, and you. You're gonna love me."

I fall back on the couch, popping the Tylenol, chugging the wine and bursting into tears.

Chapter 12

"Drake and Gabby, it's great to see the two of you again. My apologies for rescheduling last week's session."

"It's no problem. It gave us more time to finish the assignment." Gabby says handing me two envelopes. "Are you okay?"

"Yeah, I was in an accident and will be fine." I lie before opening the envelopes to scan over the documents. "I see each of you agree on finances and faith which is a great thing."

"Drake has always been great at managing money and we feel he'll be best to handle them in our household. For our faith, we believe in and serve God with all of us. Our Christianity, salvation and where we serve are equally important. Currently, we're members of my father's church and for now, it's where we plan to stay."

I jot notes before looking up at them. "Drake, where do you see your marriage in five years in relation to family?"

"I see Gabby and I happily married, traveling and enjoying each other. In year five, we'd probably slow down to prepare for children."

"Gabby, what about you?"

"Happily married for sure. However, I thought we'd start having children year four because then I'd be twenty-seven and it'll give me three years to have three children who'll all be eighteen when I turn fifty."

"Yeah but waiting until year five gives you the same timeline." Drake tells her. "Plus, I want us to experience Paris for our fifth wedding anniversary."

"Woo Paris. Okay, deal."

"Do you agree with us, doctor?" Drake questions.

"I agree with making decisions together, however have you all accounted for your plans not working?"

"What do you mean?" Gabby inquires sitting up straighter.

"What happens if the plans you've made doesn't go accordingly? What if you get pregnant on your honeymoon or in year two?"

"That won't happen." She shakes her head.

"It could."

"Not if we take measures to ensure it won't, like birth control." Gabby states getting agitated. "Why do you always try to make us second guess our answers?"

"Gabby, second guessing things isn't always bad, although it's not what I'm doing."

"Then what are you doing?" She folds her arms.

"Preparing you for a world and marriage that doesn't always go according to the plans you make. Do you think a person who gets up in the morning makes plans for an accident on their way to work or what about when you planned to have cereal, but the milk is expired?"

She looks away.

"Aren't you a party planner?" I ask her.

"Yes."

"Does everything work perfectly all the time?"

"No."

"How do you handle it when things go astray?"

"She cries." Drake answers.

"Not anymore." She nudges him. "Yes, I used to get upset when things happened but now, I learn to prevent it or plan in case it happens again."

"Because you'll be prepared, right?"

"Right."

Her eyes register what I've been trying to say.

"My point is, you have to be prepared for when things go according to your plans and when they don't. If not, you risk mishandling the times when stuff happens instead of finding a solution."

She softens. "I apologize for getting upset. I just really want our marriage to work because failure isn't an option."

"Of course, it is." I correct her. "When we think failure isn't an option, we set ourselves up to do, say and accept anything except the fact, failure can happen. When we don't allow the space to fail, we work ourselves to death, stay in loveless marriages, on dead end jobs and etc. trying to outrun failure. Only to realize, you can't."

"So, are we supposed to sit around twiddling our thumbs waiting on our marriage to fail? That's crazy."

"No." I smile at her. "You work hard to make sure it doesn't because although it's an option, it doesn't have to be what you choose."

"All of this is so confusing." Gabby admits.

"Let's say you're in college and you chose statistics. On the first day of class, the professor explains this is a hard course and there are two choices, to either pass or fail. To pass you have to attend class, participate and turn in assignments. To fail, well you don't do any of what's required. Although failing the class is an option, it isn't the one you have to choose. The same with marriage because like the class, it's hard and you have to show up, participate and turn in the assignments necessary to ensure your marriage sustains. Which will you choose?"

They look at each other.

"To put in the work." They say together.

"But how do you keep the fire burning after years of being married?" Drake inquires. "I mean, I've seen my mom and dad who are happily in love, but I know there has to be some hard times."

"Oh, there's definitely hard times, but they shouldn't be the reason you give up on marriage. To answer your question, you keep putting in the things to ensure the fire never goes out. I know it sounds simple and truth is, it is. Let's say you and Gabby go camping. At night, you start a fire to cook dinner and to stay warm. You find wood, build it and start the fire. Once the wood is burned, the fire goes out. You know why?"

"I didn't add more wood."

"Right. The fire will stay lit when it has the right amount of oxygen, the wood is stacked properly, the space to burn and it has something to burn. Drake, you can desire a certain type of marriage and have it pictured in your head from the time you understand what it means, however the only way to keep it, you have to put in the time, effort and resources to ensure it works."

"Makes sense. Thank you, Dr. Jennings."

"You're welcome and I know this is a lot to absorb seeing you're getting married in a couple of weeks, but don't allow it to overwhelm you. Doing so will make you miss the blessings of marriage instead of enjoying it. Do either of you have any questions. Great, then I'll see you next week for your final session."

When they leave, I add a few more notes to their chart and close it. Laying the iPad on the table, I lean my head back remembering the time I foolishly thought love was enough.

"Mom, I hear you, but Harvey and I love each other."

"Little girl, if love was enough there'd be no need for divorce lawyers. Marriage isn't only about love, that's what the Bible says we're supposed to give each other. Wondah, your marriage survives when you like each other too because liking each other will get you through the times when the love becomes ordinary. Love may create the marriage but liking each other bonds the friendship."

A tap on the door brings me out of my thoughts.

"Hey," Angelique says. "You okay?"

"Angel, what are you doing here?" I ask getting ready to stand.

"No, don't get up. I was on my way home, decided to stop through to see how you are since you won't answer my calls and judging by the boot and stitches on your head, I can surmise not good."

"Are you here as a friend or therapist?"

"Um, your friend who happens to be a therapist." She shrugs.

Chuckling, my breath catches in my throat as tears fall. She pulls up a chair, grabbing my hand.

"I wish Harvey would have died." I admit.

Chapter 13

"You don't mean that." Angelique says.

"I do with my whole heart. At least then I'd have some sort of understanding for this pain because right now it doesn't make sense."

"Sometimes the things we endure aren't for understanding but to stretch our faith. We always use the story of Job, but God offered Job because of his countenance, character and conscience. God himself said Job was blameless, upright, fears God and shuns evil. Job didn't understand, but God was banking on his faith being just as strong in Him during the bad as it was when all was good."

"No offense, but I don't want to hear this. The flesh of me is hurting and stretching my faith isn't priority because the only thing I want to do is stretch my hand and hurt Harvey. What else I don't understand is why God would allow me to be blindsided by this when He gives warnings about everything else."

"Would it have mattered?"

I look at her.

"What would a warning have done differently? You'd still be in this place of hurt."

"Yeah, but it would have been better than walking into the kitchen to divorce papers and a husband who acts like his feelings dissolved." I bellow.

She touches my hand. "I didn't mean to upset you."

"And I didn't mean to yell. It's just, I thought I knew my husband but I'm starting to think it was me I didn't know. How else could I allow myself to be caught off guard like this? I've prepared couples for marriage, counseled people through divorce, infidelity and the spark going out, etc. yet I never prepared for it to happen to me. I'm a marriage counselor who couldn't save her own marriage."

"Girl do surgeons operate on themselves? No, because looking through the eyes of a physician instead of patient stops them from seeing the problem correctly."

"Are you saying this is my fault?"

"Sis remove the sass from your voice because I don't scare easily and that's not what I said. Wondah, can you honestly say even if you'd seen a problem, you would have reached out for help?"

"That's not the point." I state.

"So, the answer is no."

"What are you getting at?"

"You couldn't control Harvey and regardless if there was something you missed, you can't do anything about it now. Your marriage is over, and it hurts. You didn't have a say in it, and it sucks. However, you do have a say in what happens next and after you've grieved, cried, thrown fits, destroyed cars and whatever else; what's next because you can't stay in this place and neither can you go back. What's next?"

"I don't know," I yell knocking my crutch over, "and I'm not ready to figure it out. It's been twenty-seven days. I think I deserve to be angry a little while longer."

"No one is rushing you to get through this because everyone's grief process is different. Nonetheless, we both know anger leaves room for the enemy. Your enemy, at the moment, is you."

"I'm not your patient Angelique."

"No, you're my best friend whom I love and patient or not, anger hasn't been good to you."

"Well, it's all I got to sleep with at the moment." She sighs.

"Angel, none of you understand what this is like for me. I invested everything I had into our marriage and family and now I feel like my account has been depleted. I feel empty and I don't know who I am without them."

"Sure, you do. I've known you for over fifteen years and you may have some problems, but an identity crisis isn't one of them. You simply have to survive the anger long enough to see you again. Now, come on."

"Where are we going?"

"To release some of this pent-up anger." She says holding out her hand to me.

"Release? What is this place?" I ask Angelique when we arrive at a building.

"It's a gym."

You brought me to a gym? Uh, you do see this boot, right?"

"This isn't your ordinary gym and they'll work around it."

"I don't have any workout clothes."

"Just come on."

"Angel, hey, I wasn't expecting to see you tonight." A young lady says when we walk through the doors.

"AJ, this is my best friend Wondah and she has plenty that needs to be released tonight."

"Then you've come to the right place. Hi Wanda, my name is Antoinette, but everyone calls me AJ."

"It's Wondah," I spell out. "It's similar but different."

"No need to explain, your name has meaning, and you should correct it when someone gets it wrong." She tells me.

"Thanks, and it's nice to meet you."

She smiles. "You say that now. Follow me."

I look back at Angelique who motions for me to go.

"Wondah, what's the first thing most people do when they get to the gym?" she questions.

"Change clothes."

"Do you know why?"

"The clothes they have on may not be appropriate for working out." I answer.

"That's true because clothes designed for exercise allows your body to breathe while causing the sweat to evaporate. However, I also believe changing your clothes mentally prepares you for the workout. Some experts call it *enclothed cognition*, stating your mental shifts when you wear certain clothes."

We stop in front of a door with a sign, Locker Room. She pushes the door open and I walk inside to see a huge message on the wall ... NO MATTER WHAT, I'M _____

"Why the blank line?" I question.

"You decide how it ends. For me, it changes daily. Today, it's no matter what I'm enough. What's yours?"

"No matter what," I pause. "No matter what, I'm capable."

"Why capable?"

"It means I have the ability even though I may not have the strength." I tell her as my eyes fill with tears.

She leads me to a bench.

"Wondah, we start in the locker room not to change clothes, but to change your perspective on whatever it is you've brought here to release. Here in the locker room, it's your safe space to undress mentally without the worry of judgment or shame. In this room, you can take off as much or as little you decide. If you look around, you'll see there are no lockers. This is because we aren't keeping anything that doesn't need to be kept. What you shed in this room, it's for your freedom because no matter what, you're capable."

"My mouth says I'm capable while my mind is saying I'm a fool."

"Why do you believe you're a fool?" she asks.

"A few weeks ago, my husband of twenty-seven years presented me with divorce papers on my fiftieth birthday."

"Were you in agreement with it?"

I chuckle. "In agreement? I had no idea he even wanted one. Oh, this was after we stayed up making love the night before. So, no I was not in agreement, but I am angry."

"You have every right to be and being here tonight isn't trying to force you into believing otherwise."

"Then what's the point?"

"To give you healthier ways of releasing the anger."

"Angelique must have told you—

"No," she interjects. "Angel hasn't told me anything about you, however I know firsthand the danger of divorce regardless of who's at fault, who asked for it or how long it takes. Divorce is dangerous emotionally, mentally, physically and financially because it can leave you in a dark place and without help, you might not make it out of. Why do you think I opened this gym? Baby, I was so angry after my divorce I needed a place to release the rage or I would be doing life in prison after smiling on my mugshot."

She plasters on a huge grin and we both laugh.

"Seriously, Wondah I was in a dark headspace and I knew if I didn't release myself from it, I wouldn't have survived and quite possibly could've taken others with me. I needed a release and through the pain, God would allow Release to be birth. An unordinary place to escape the confinement of doubt, fear, shame, anger, restrictions and everything else. My only prayer is for this place to help you heal more than it did me."

"I don't know if I'm ready to release it. Don't get me wrong, I know I need to, but I think after twenty-seven years with one Negro, I deserve time to be angry."

"You absolutely do, however how far has anger gotten you lately?" she probes.

I look at her.

"You don't have to answer, but will you at least release a little before you leave?"

"Sure."

"Great."

She gets up and comes back with tape. I look at her with curiosity.

"Angel didn't tell you, did she?"

"Tell me what?"

"Here at Release, we box it out."

After getting home, I fall onto the couch. Although I was sitting the entire time I boxed, it was still a workout.

"Okay Wondah, punch this bag with all your might."

I swing.

"Come on girl, I know you got more than that penned inside."

"Ah," I scream and swing again.

"Punch like you're freeing yourself."

I swing again, harder.

"Punch like it's your last time and your life is on the line."

I swing again.

"Punch like this next one is the release you need to be free."

I wipe the tears falling as I punch the pillows of the couch.

"Why wasn't I enough?" I question myself.

Chapter 14

"Hey sis, how are you feeling?" Denise asks walking into the exam room.

"I'd be better when I can put pressure on this foot." I tell her. "It's been long enough, right?"

"Let me take a look." She sits in front of me removing the bandage. "Does this hurt?"

"A little."

She pokes a few more places.

"You're actually healing faster than I expected and your stitches have completely dissolved. Stand for me."

She helps me up and after a few minutes, I'm able to balance.

"How does it feel?'

"It feels okay."

"It's been almost three weeks, so you will have some discomfort when standing. Did you bring your other shoe?"

"It's in my bag."

She gets it and helps to put it on. "Okay, when you're ready I want you to take a few steps. It's going to feel weird after being on crutches, but I think you're ready."

I put pressure on the foot.

"You okay?" she asks when I don't move.

"Yeah," I reply. "Just mentally preparing." Taking a deep breath, I take the first step.

"Is there any sharp or shooting pain when you walk?"

"Nope."

"Good, then you can officially retire the crutches, but I still want you to take it easy for the next couple of weeks which means no heels until the pain is completely gone."

"Thank God."

"Speaking of God, why haven't you been to church?" Denise questions while cleaning up the room.

"I watch the service online."

"It's not the same."

"Denise, please don't start. It's only been one Sunday."

"Three, actually." She corrects.

"Well, stop counting because my salvation or lack thereof is between me and God. Besides, I think He understands."

"Are you really pulling the He knows my heart card?"

I shrug.

"Wondah, you may not want to hear this, but I'm going to say it anyway. Yes, God knows your heart, but He also validates your motives and actions. It's like giving your keys to the valet. Sure, they may know you and your car, however the only way you'll get the keys is with your ticket."

"That's not the same and you know it."

"You get the point. Sister, I know you're hurting, grieving and probably feeling every emotion under the sun and stars however, this isn't the time to turn away from God."

"I never said I was turning away from Him and missing a couple of Sundays doesn't void my spirituality Denise. I'm not going to church, I didn't say I wasn't going to God. Shoot, if it wasn't for God, I don't know how I'd survived these last thirty-two days."

"You're keeping count?" she asks.

"I sure am."

"Why?"

"Because Nina, my lawyer, says it takes sixty days to finalize the divorce and I'm giving myself that long to get this Negro out of my system."

"Are you prepared if it takes longer?"

I roll my eyes.

"What? You can't handle taking your own advice?" she laughs.

"Whatever. Can I go now?"

"Yes, but will you at least come out with us tomorrow night? The girls and I miss you."

"You're going to miss Bible study, Mrs. Prim & Proper?"

"Hush. Will you or not?"

"Where?"

"There's a new Blues club opening downtown called Melodies. Chad and his band are headlining."

"Sharda's husband Chad?"

"Yes. See, you'd be in the know if you responded to our group messages."

"I'll think about it." I tell her.

"Fine. Now, turn the freaking notifications back on because you've missed some juicy gossip in the text thread."

"Just because I haven't responded, it doesn't mean I didn't read them." I lick my tongue at her on the way out the door.

"Heifer." I hear her mumble and I laugh.

The next afternoon, I'm sitting in the office going over notes from my last session when the door bursts open.

"He's gone." Kimberley cries. "This is all your fault."

"Wondah, I'm sorry. I tried to stop her." Asha rushes in.

"It's okay. Can you grab a bottle of water for her." I get up and go over to my client. "Kim, you're upset but you need to calm down and tell me what's going on."

"Don't tell me to calm down. Hudson left me." She seethes. "I thought coming here would save my marriage and instead, I find a freaking Dear John letter waiting for me at home. You were supposed to fix us."

"Girl, I'm a marriage counselor, not a miracle worker."

"This isn't a joke." She yells.

"And nothing I've said should have been taken as one. Kim, you burst into my office casting blame for a marriage only you were trying to save. I told you last week—

"I know what you said but what am I supposed to do Dr. Jennings?" she exclaims. "He was my everything."

I wait until she calms a little. "No, you made him your everything. Take a seat."

Asha comes back with the water and gives it to her.

"Dr. Jennings, I don't know what I did wrong."

"What makes you think you did anything wrong?" I question.

"Why else would he leave me?"

"Because he could."

She stops mid sip of the water.

"It hurts to hear, huh? However, the truth is, nobody needs a reason to leave. It's a choice. The same way you chose to do everything for him even though he never appreciated it. You cooked, cleaned, stayed in shape, wore your hair the way he likes and even dressed in what he told you and he still left. You know why?"

"Because he could." She sobs into her hand. "I'm such a fool."

"I thought the same thing about myself here recently until God woke me up the other night and I searched this word called fool. Interestingly enough, there are three kinds of people God calls fools. One who doesn't believe in God, one who mocks sin and one who isn't prepared to die. I don't think you or I fall into that category."

"I just, I don't know Dr. Jennings." She shakes her head. "I believed us coming here would sustain our marriage."

"Why? Did he give you any indication it would? In every session he was disconnected and no matter how hard you pushed, this could only work if he put in the effort."

"It hurts."

"I know and it's going to take time to get over, but here's what I need you to do for me. Faith it. Even though your marriage failed, your faith shouldn't. When people fail us, our faith doesn't. When promises are broken, our faith is still intact because Bible tells us in Hebrews ten and thirty-nine," I stop to grab my iPad. "It says actually starting at thirty-eight, *"And my righteous ones will live by faith. But I will take no pleasure in anyone who turns away. But we are not like those who turn away from God to their own destruction. We are the faithful ones, whose souls will be saved."* You may know this next verse, but it says, *"Now faith is the substance of things hoped for, the evidence of things not seen."*"

She cries, and I have to catch myself from joining her.

"Kim, you're stronger than you know." I clear my throat to stop the emotions threatening to seep out. "Hudson walked away from you, but it doesn't mean you won't survive. Even the strongest, tallest and most beautiful trees lose their leaves, yet it doesn't stop them from growing and neither does it take away their strength or identity. It's simply shedding the leaves to conserve resources until it's time for it to blossom again. Take this as your season to shed, knowing you'll bloom again."

She stands. "Thank you, Dr. Jennings."

"You're welcome and Kim, divorce didn't take your identity, you simply need to believe in who you are again."

When she leaves out, I let the tears fall.

"Are you okay?" Asha asks from the doorway.

"No, I think I need to take my own advice." I smile through my tears.

Chapter 15

I rush home to shower and change. Deciding on jeans and tank top, I head out to meet the gang. I decided to take an Uber because I didn't know what the parking is like at Melodies. Getting out, I press send on a text to Denise at the same time she calls my name.

"I'm glad you came."

"Auntie," Sharda squeals when I walk in. "Thank you for coming."

I hug her and everyone else in attendance.

"Good evening, may I get you something to drink?" the young man asks.

"I'll take a strawberry Hennessy if you have it on the menu."

"Be right back."

The lights dim, and when the stage lights go on, everyone cheers.

"Good evening." A lady bellows from the microphone. "Thank you for joining us on the opening night of Melodies, Memphis' newest and upcoming spot for music and entertainment. Tonight, we are excited to welcome the first band to bless this stage. Put your hands together for Highway 901."

"Really?" I ask Sharda. "That's the best they could come up with?"

"It was better than the other choices." She shrugs and laughs.

"How y'all feeling tonight?" Chad says over the mic. "We are Highway 901 and we've come to entertain, not talk. Ready boys."

The drummer counts it off as the music to Sam Cooke's, "A Change is Gonna Come" begins. When Chad belts out the first stance, everybody goes wild.

"That's my man." Sharda screams.

The waiter sits my drink in front of me.

"Thanks. Go on and put in another."

"Now, let's have some real fun." Chad says before singing "I'm Trapped" by Carl Sims.

"Okay," I holler out. "I'm trapped, I'm caught up in the middle of a two-way love affair." I sing with him.

An hour and half plus a few drinks later, I'm dancing in my chair to Lattimore's "Let's Straighten it Out."

"You been tossin and turnin in yo sleep lately, just sittin round poutin all day long. Now how in the hell you expect me to understand when I don't even know what's wrong." Chad is serenading Sharda.

"Oh, he knows girl. Fuck him." I scream, and everyone laughs.

"Let's straighten it out." Chad continues. "Man, what a night." He says into the microphone. "Before we close this set, I cannot leave here without introducing the members of the band."

When he's done, he calls Sharda up to help him with the last song.

"Hurting inside. Simply because it takes a lot of strength to say goodbye, Oh, it's so hard to do. I wonder if I'm wrong, I thought the whole thing over and I still can't tell you why. It's gone. Baby, I can't accept the pain that we bring, that we bring to each other. There's nothing to gain from hurting one another, so I'm walking in the rain looking for the strength to say goodbye." Chad sings staring at his wife.

Sharda closes her eyes as she grips the microphone and sings. "My man, I want to call you and say it's on again. It's not like I don't love you, I don't love you any more I thought the whole thing over and it's not like it was before."

"Okay, I'm out." I stand and grab my purse.

"Wondah, wait." Denise runs behind me. "Let me take you home."

"No, stay and enjoy the rest of the night."

"It's cool, I need to leave anyway because I have an early morning and Daniel and I are in separate cars."

"Nise, you don't have to leave on my account. I'm good."

"Girl hush and come on."

Pulling in front of the house, I sit in the passenger's seat staring at the door.

"There used to be a time I'd be happy to pull up at this house and now all it brings is pain."

Denise squeezes my hand and I turn to look at her.

"Thank you for getting me out the house tonight. I needed it more than I realized."

"You know what else you need?"

"A man."

"A man? Girl, I was going to say a sleepover."

"Right with a man."

"You know what, get out of my car." She laughs. "Friday, I'm coming over for a sleepover, so be prepared."

"Yes ma'am. Text me when you make it home. Be safe and I love you."

"I love you too."

Once inside, I arm the alarm, grab a bottle of water from the refrigerator and head for the bedroom. Standing in the middle of the room, I look around and although the color of the walls changed, and the furniture is different, everything reminds me of him. It doesn't matter he walked out thirty-three days ago, he's still here. I touch my chest where my heart resides because he's still there too, no matter the amount of disdain I hold towards him.

"Why can't I move forward?"

I scream.

Hours later, I'm sitting in the middle of the bed holding my journal. The page has captured the majority of my tears and it seems they will not stop.

I wipe my hand across the paper for the third time. Picking up the pen, I close my eyes before beginning to write.

Thursday, May 14th, 2020.

3:10 AM.

Suicide.

The action of killing oneself intentionally.

I've been sitting here for hours and the only word that keeps ringing through my head is suicide. I won't lie and say it hasn't been a thought, it has. Not because dude left me, I will NOT give him the satisfaction nor the tears to cry over me. Suicide was a thought because it's a way for this pain to end. A pain I didn't even know one person could cause by choosing to walk away. A pain that runs so deep, I feel it in the tips of my toes. How is it even possible when it's just a marriage, right? No! It's not JUST a marriage. It was a vow, a promise, a purpose, a plan, a commitment, a lifetime ... and in a moment, it's all gone.

I shake my hand to relieve the pain writing has caused before I start back.

What's next?

What's next for me?

How do I move on?

How do I forget everything?

Am I supposed to?

I stop and lean back against the headboard, closing my eyes. A few seconds later, they pop open.

"Maybe you aren't supposed to forget." I sit back up.

Maybe I'm not supposed to forget. What if I'm supposed to forgive?

Shaking my head. "This is going to be harder than I thought."

Chapter 16

Sitting at my desk, at the office, circling June 16th with a bright red marker because according to my lawyer, it's the day of the divorce hearing.

"Hey," Asha says from the door. "The Clarkes are here to pick up their official certificate for the completion of their premarital counseling and they'd like a word with you."

"Sure, send them in. Gabby and Drake, is everything okay?"

"Yes." She beams and hands me a card. "We wanted to thank you for all your help and officially invite you to the wedding."

"You're welcome and congratulations. I pray you both have an enjoyable, happy, healthy, loving, communicable, prayer and God filled marriage. May God's hands forever be upon your union and may you always keep Him first."

She rushes over and hugs me.

"We will. Thank you, Dr. Jennings."

I watch them walk out hand in hand. A few minutes later Asha returns.

"Are you going to the wedding?"

"No, I don't like to cross the boundary of doctor/patient, but can you send a gift card or something on my behalf."

"Of course. Is there anything else you need me to do before I head out?"

"Nope, I only have a few more notes to finish and then I'm out of here. My sister has threatened me into having a girls night in."

"It sounds like fun."

"For who?" I laugh. "All she wants to do is be all up in my business."

"Aren't this what sisters are for?"

"Whose side are you on?"

She giggles. "You might enjoy it."

"We'll see. Have a great weekend Asha and I'll see you on Monday."

Three hours later, I'm in the kitchen dancing and singing to Mel Waiters, "Hole in the Wall" while pouring chips into a bowl for the dip Isabel fixed and left in the refrigerator.

"Let's go baby to the hole in the wall. I've had my best time y'all at the hole in the wall. I took my high-class woman with me the next night. She didn't want to get out of the car, she said it didn't look right. She walked into the room with her nose in the air, it's seven in the morning y'all and she's still in there. Smoke filled room, whiskey and chicken wings. People dancing and drinking, and no one wants to leave."

I turn and jump at the sight of Angelique and Denise.

"Mother—why are y'all sneaking up on me?" I grab my phone and stop the music.

"No, please don't stop on the count of us." Denise laughs.

"If you didn't have the music blasting while dancing around like this is an old juke joint, you would have heard us." Angel laughs mimicking my dance moves.

I throw a pretzel at her. "Hush. I'm mentally preparing to stay up all night with you two old hens."

"Don't forget me." Sharda sings coming in.

"They roped you into this too." I say giving her a hug.

"Auntie, my bag was packed ten minutes after Denise called. There was no way I'm missing a night without a husband and children."

We all laugh.

"Then let's get this party started." Angel bellows.

"Wait. I know you didn't come up in here without my non-porker delight pizza from Broadway?" I turn to her.

"Pizza? Was I supposed to get pizza?" she feigns confusion.

"Heifer, don't make me black your eye."

"Girl, it's already in the living room."

A little while later, we're sprawled across the living room floor full, drinking and laughing.

"Okay ladies, it's time for a game." Sharda says already borderline tipsy as she lines the table with shot glasses. "This game is called Truth and Lies."

"Aw hell." We all say together.

"It's fun, I promise. Each person has to tell two things about themselves, one true and the other a lie. The player on your left has to determine which one is true and if she's wrong, she has to drink. If she gets it right, the person who told the story has to drink. See, fun and I'll go first." She plops down. "Number one. I've been going back to school for the last three months to get my doctorate and I'm having an affair with my professor. Number two. Some days when I need some alone time, I slip melatonin into Chad and the kids' sweet tea with dinner."

"Damn," Denise laughs. "Um, I'm going to say number one is true."

"What? No." Sharda squeals.

"Girl, we all know number two is true, I just needed a drink and you were taking too long."

We burst into laughing.

"Wait," she says folding her arms. "Why is it hard to believe I wasn't freaking a professor?"

"Sharda, we know you and you'd never cheat on Chad." I tell her.

"I want too." She whispers into the pillow.

"You what?" Angel screams.

"I didn't mean it like that." She sighs. "Okay, hear me out. There are times when I think about Idris Elba or the fine dude at the gym bending me over in the weight room. I mean, who doesn't after being married for so long, but I'd never act on them though. In fact, I use those fantasies to keep our sex life lit."

"Have you ever told Chad?" I ask her.

"Yes, of course. We have open dialogue about our sex life the same way we do about the kids and finances because it matters."

"Yeah, until those thoughts turn into action and your marriage is over." I rebut.

"Okay, my turn." Denise states. "Number one."

"Hold on, D. Wondah, when I say I sometimes fantasize about other men, that's all it is. A fantasy. Hell, I've had three children, my boobs hang like footlong hotdogs and my stomach isn't as flat as it used to be. I've been married to the same man for twelve years and although he calls me sexy, I still find myself dreaming another man thinks I am too. It doesn't mean my self-esteem is low or I need reassuring, but damnit it feels good. When the fantasy is over, I go home and slut my husband out in our bedroom."

The room is silent.

"Footlong hotdogs, really?" Denise says, and we all laugh. Sharda grabs her breast.

"Like the ones from Sonic."

Chapter 17

"I'm sorry." I say once the laughter has died down. "I shouldn't have said that. It's just, I'm sorry." Tears fill my eyes.

"Wondah." Denise soberly says.

"It's okay. Give me a shot so I can get out of my head."

"No, tell us what's going on." Angel orders grabbing my hand. "We've allowed you space to grieve in your own way, but we're here. Talk to us and stop holding all this in."

I squeeze the pillow I'm holding. "I don't know." I cry. "Some days, I feel as though I can get through this and I'll be alright. Then night comes, and I feel like I'll never be the same."

"You won't be the same." Angel states. "Wondah, you're going through a divorce from the man you've spent most of your life with. It's bound to change things about the way you live. However, you have to decide how this change affects you and the remaining life you have left. You can't do this with anger riding as your passenger."

"Angel is right, and you don't have to be strong for us because we love you even the times you are a crying mess." Denise assures me.

"I'm not trying to be strong, I'm trying to survive and in order to do it, I have to get up every day even though my heart is broken. I have to continue on with life as normal because if I don't and I lay in my anger too long, it might not let me go." I shake my head and let the tears fall. "My body feels like I've been thrown around in a car that's been flipped a hundred times. My mind is in a constant fog because I can't make sense of how I went to bed married and woke up to divorce. My habits haven't changed even though my husband did. I come home prepared to cook dinner and then I remember, it's only me. I walk inside his closet to get the laundry hamper and then

I remember, it's only me. I roll over in the middle of the night, expecting to hit a warm body, but then I remember, it's only me. And," I shake my head again. "And no matter what I do, the hurt and pain will not release me. It won't."

Angel gets up on her knees, wrapping her arms around me.

"It won't stop." I grab her arms and allow the pain to release from my belly. "Oh God."

Denise and Sharda crawl over to where we are, placing their hands on me as Angel begins to pray.

"Father, I come petitioning your throne of infinite power, wisdom, strength and mercy asking you to hear the plea of your daughter. God, as I speak, move in the heart of my sister Wondah for it's her who needs you. She needs strength to survive the grief she's been thrust into. She needs your comfort for the nights confusion toils with her mind. She needs your peace when anger has intertwined itself into her plans. She needs guidance when guilt is leading her astray. She needs you, Father. While we don't understand, we trust there has to be glory after this. Until then, give her what she needs to heal. Then God, for the times when she's weak, strengthen us to carry her. When she feels as though she can't go on, give us a listening ear and a strong shoulder to lend her to cry on. While she heals, I pray you'll keep her mind, body, soul and spirit. The enemy is trying to use pain to hinder her, but he's a liar. Wondah's identity is in you God. Father, it shall be well. This I pray. Amen."

I'm rocking back and forth.

"Like Moses said in Deuteronomy thirty, verse nineteen," Denise says grabbing my chin to lift my head. *"Today I have given you the choice between life and death, between blessings and curses. Now I call on heaven and earth to witness the choice you make. Oh, that you would choose life, so that you and your descendants might live!"* You have to live sister. You have to live healthy, happy and restored because I can't lose my big sister."

"And we won't rush you to heal, take all the time you need, but come back to us." Sharda tells me with tears streaming. "Come back to me because I can't imagine life without you."

"I'm trying."

Sharda begins to sing. "In the middle of the turbulence surrounding you, these trying times that are so hard to endure. In the middle of what seems to be your darkest hour, hold fast your heart and be assured. This too shall pass. Like every night that's come before it, He'll never give you more than you can bear. This too shall pass so in this thought be comforted. It's in His Hands. This too shall pass."

We stay hugged for a few minutes.

"Nothing can get you back to God quicker than whiskey, heart break and a tipsy gospel singer." I chuckle and wipe my face. "You all turned girl's night into revival and I'm here for it."

"Really Wondah?" Denise rolls her eyes.

"Girl, forget you." Sharda pushes me and laughs. "I sounded good."

"Seriously. Thank you all. Neither of you hesitated to pray for me and because you did, I feel some weight has been lifted from me. Y'all, I never knew how heavy anger could be until it became my daily baggage to carry."

"Sad reality, this is when most of us realize it." Angel tells me. "Yet, here's what I've learned. Anger can do one of two things. It can force you into becoming something better or it'll turn you into someone bitter. You have to choose."

"Dang Dr. Angel is spitting knowledge tonight." Sharda says snapping her fingers. "I'll drink to that."

"You don't need to drink to nothing else."

"Baby, I'm taking full advantage of this night and half of tomorrow. So, pour up and let's get back to this game. Denise, your turn."

Hours later, Angel and Denise are in the guest rooms and Sharda is sprawled across the couch, on her stomach with her nightgown raised exposing all of her assets. I snap a picture, as payback, before trying to wake her to get in the bed. When those attempts are unsuccessful, I throw a blanket over her and turn out the lights.

I go into my bedroom and close the door. Getting into bed with my phone, I open the Facebook app. Clicking search, I see Harvey Jennings as the first name in the search bar and Anette Taylor as the second.

"No." I say out loud. "I can't keep doing this to myself." I erase my search history, block him and her before logging into the fake page I created and deleting it. "Lord, free me from this."

Chapter 18

Saturday afternoon, the ladies and I are on the patio with music playing, mimosas being poured and cigars.

"This is a great cigar." Denise pulls it from her lips and admire it. "Where did you get it from?"

"I met this lady at a vendor event earlier this year. Her business is called Chicks & Cigars. You need to check her out."

"I'm definitely getting Daniel some of these."

"This is my jam." Sharda squeals jumping up when the music to "She's a Bad Mama Jama" by Carl Carlton begins to play.

We all begin to sing.

"She's a bad mama jama, just as fine as she can be. Her body measurements are perfect in every dimension. She's got a figure that's sure enough getting attention. She's poetry in motion, a beautiful sight to see. I get so excited viewing her anatomy. She's built, oh, she's stacked. Got all the curves that men like."

When Sharda stops mid dance, we turn to see Harvey standing at the bottom of the stairs. I turn the music down.

"Um, why are you letting yourself into this lady's house?" she asks him.

"I rang the doorbell." He flatly responds.

"If there was no answer you should have taken your bobblehead ass on." Angelique tells him.

"Harvey, what do you need?" I ask causing them to turn to me.

"I tried to call. I need to get some paperwork from the office."

"No need to explain. Get whatever you need and go."

They all look at me and I shrug. "What? I'm no longer allowing him to dictate how I react to his ugly ass." I turn the music volume back up.

Sunday morning, I walk into the sanctuary of the church as the devotion is ending. The praise leader begins to sing a slow song repeating the lyrics, I trust you Lord. By the time the song is over, the church is still in worship.

"Oh, come on, this is a great place to tell the Lord, I'll trust you." Minister Franklin says. "Anybody got a Lord, I'll trust you even when I don't know what to do praise? Lord, I'll trust you even when it hurts me to the core. Lord, I'll trust you when I can't even see my way because I know you haven't left me. Anybody other than me got a praise this morning."

"Whatever your will is Lord, I trust you." Patrick, the praise leader sings behind him. "I trust you. I may not understand it, but I trust you. Don't know what way to go, but I trust you."

"I trust you Lord." I cry out with my hands lifted. "Direct me Lord and I'll go. Yes, Lord. Whatever you have for me to do, I'll do. I trust you."

After offering and prayer, Pastor Jordan walks to the pulpit.

"Whew, the spirit of the Lord is in this place this morning. Lord, we thank you and I trust you. Have your way in this place and in your messenger. God, allow your spirit to become greater than my flesh that I may speak the words you've been marinating in my belly. God, I've prepared for this moment and yet I cannot do it without you. Move by your might and settle here. This I pray, amen."

"Amen."

"Turn with me in your Bibles to Psalm 46. When you have it, stand all over the room in reverence of God's word."

She pauses to give time. Once the majority is standing, she proceeds.

"The word of God reads in verses one through three, *"God is our refuge and strength, a very present help in trouble. Therefore, we will not fear, even though the earth be removed, and though the mountains be carried into the midst of the sea; though its waters roar and be troubled, though the mountains shake with its swelling. Selah."* For a moment of your time, my subject is chaotic world, calm God.

Have you ever found yourself in the midst of mess because you allowed chaos to enter and common-sense to exit? Maybe you haven't, but I've made mistakes because I allowed chaos and confusion to dictate decisions instead of God. I've been overly emotional and lashed out at people who were trying to help. Why? Because again, when chaos enters, common sense goes out the window.

But what if God didn't keep His cool? What if His anger towards us burned immediately after we did something stupid? What if God, when faced with chaos, didn't control His emotions? What do you think would happen if we lived in a chaotic world with a God who couldn't remain calm under pressure? Sure, we've all faced trials and troubles, seen our share of sickness and death yet one thing has remained the same. God is our refuge and strength, a very present help in trouble.

Here's what I like about the author of Psalm 46. He didn't start with his problems, he began with a solution. For he tells us, God is our refuge and strength, a very present help in trouble. See, I can imagine the author while penning these sweet words thinking, one day somebody will read this who knows about trouble because they've experienced pain, had some sleepless nights, some days filled with uncertainty, dealt with the agony of death, seen sickness, been lied on, abused, let down, hurt, did some things they aren't proud of, had some moments of wanting to leave everybody and everything so, I don't need to remind them of tribulations. Instead, I'll bring to their remembrance God. Letting them know God is still God.

God, our refuge and strength. God, who is beginning and end. God, creator of life. God, sustainer and way maker. God, who is peace and joy. God, who is light in darkness. He says, I don't need to remind them of all the hell they've had to endure, I'll let them know the author of our faith, God, is still crafting our stories of testimonies.

He says, I don't need to remind you of the destruction, you lived it so let me bring to your remembrance the deliverer. I don't need to retell the story of how you almost lost your mind, you were there but let me give you hope. I don't need to tell you about the darkness, you lived it. So, instead let me recap for you the man who is known as the bright and morning star. Yeah, I know you've been through hell but baby, don't lose hope yet because I know a man whom I describe as our refuge and strength, a very present help in the time of trouble.

This author says, I don't need to tell them about trouble, they're familiar with him but let me remind them of who God is so when they face trouble again, they'll know who to call. When the world gets too chaotic, they'll know who to trust. When times get hard and the burdens of life are becoming too heavy to bear alone, he says, I'll remind them even in the midst of a chaotic world, we serve a calm God."

After the soul stirring sermon by Pastor Jordan, I'm happy I chose to attend service in person because I needed it. Once outside the doors, Harvey rushes up to me.

"Why did you tell Pastor Jordan my business?" he whispers in my face with anger.

"Hold up lil fella, you need to take a step back. Now, what are you talking about?"

"Pastor Jordan has asked me to step down from the deacon board because of my situation with Anette."

"Okay and that has what to do with me?" I ask with my face scrunched in confusion.

"You had no right to tell her anything."

"Number a, I don't give a flying flip about you and your statutory rape case. Number b, I didn't tell anybody anything because well, refer to number a. Your whoring around is not my concern sweet pea. Take care or don't, I could care less either way. However, you won't steal my joy today or ever SATAN." I emphasize before pushing pass him to my car humming the song from devotion while I decide where to eat brunch.

Chapter 19

The last two weeks have been a blur. Although I haven't been drinking like I was, sleep has still been hard to come. I've tried praying, listening to music, playing games on my phone, writing in my journal and warm milk. Nothing works because I can't seem to turn off my mind. Usually, I'm laying awake staring at the ceiling, overthinking. Like tonight. Well, morning because it's 4:22 AM on Memorial Day and no matter what I do, I cannot keep my eyes closed long enough to fall into a deep sleep.

"Maybe I should try weed." I say out loud. "But where would I get it from? It's not like I can walk up to someone on the corner and ask." I laugh. "Wondah, you're losing it girl."

My cell phone rings on the nightstand scaring me. I quickly turn over, reaching to get it. It's Denise.

"Sis, what's wrong? Hello."

"Wondah," the phone breaks up. "There's—accident—and—"

"Denise, your phone is breaking up." The call drops.

I try calling her back, but it goes straight to voicemail. I try again, twice before sending a text.

Me: Sis, please call me back. Where are you? Are you okay?

I sit up in the bed, my heart racing as all kinds of things begin to go through my head. I throw the cover back to get up when an unknown number comes across the screen.

"Denise," I answer.

"Yeah, it's me. Listen. There's been an accident and you need to get to Regional One."

"Nise, slow down. Regional One? Oh my God, is it Daniel, Sharda, who?" I frantically ask.

She takes a deep breath. "Wait, no I'm sorry." She pauses.

"Then who is it? Nise, tell me what's going on."

"Its Harvey."

"Harvey? Girl, shit. I thought you were talking about somebody I'd actually get up for. Forget him. No thank you." I say climbing back in the bed.

"Wondah, listen to me. It's bad and you need to get here."

"That man is not my husband anymore. Call his pregnant fiancé."

"I know the situation of your relationship, but for all legal purposes you're still officially Mrs. Harvey Jennings until the judge declares otherwise, so get your ass here now."

She hangs up and I contemplate ignoring her. Then I think of Haven. I pick up the phone to call her and decide to wait until I know what's going on.

I look up towards the ceiling, kicking my legs against the sheets. "Really God, on day 51? Ugh."

*****

"Patient's name?" the rude lady barks when I walk up to the desk.

"Harvey Jennings."

"You are?"

"His wife."

"I'll need some id."

I hand it to her. Two minutes later, she hands it back with a visitor's badge.

"Um, where do I go?"

"Through those doors, make a right and you'll see security. They can direct you to the trauma bay. Next."

Walking through the double doors, Denise and another man is waiting.

"Wondah, this is Dr. Cartwright and he's overseeing Harvey's care. Alonzo, this is my sister Wondah."

"Dr. Cartwright," I say holding out my hand.

"Wondah, your husband was out in the field doing volunteer work when the ambulance he was in was hit by an 18-wheeler. Because he was in the back, he was thrown around and suffered a lot of damage, including some burns to his leg after the rig caught fire." Dr. Cartwright states.

"Oh God."

"He's alive." Denise tells me.

"Is this the good news?" I ask.

"Uh, yes." Dr. Cartwright stumbles.

"Don't pay her any mind." Denise rolls her eyes in my direction. "Go on."

"Your husband is going to have months of recovery. Right now, he's stable but he suffered a broken pelvis, ribs, a dislocated right jaw and burns covering most of his right leg. He'll be going into surgery within the next few minutes. If you'd like to see him, Dr. Dae can show you where he is, and I'll come speak to you when we're done."

"Thank you, Dr. Cartwright."

When he walks off Denise turns to me.

"I know this is hard, but you're that man's wife and the only one who can make decisions regarding his care."

"Haven is grown."

"Wondah, don't put this burden on that baby. Not right now. Get him through the surgery first. Please." She begs. "Do it for me."

"Fine, but then I'm out and I don't care what happens to him." I begin to walk even though I have no clue where I'm going.

She grabs my arm, leading me to some double doors.

"He's sedated and probably won't respond to you."

"Good."

Getting to the door of Trauma Bay 7, she pauses before pushing it open. Walking in, the sight of the chaos that took place before I arrived stops me. There's blood, bandages, towels, empty syringes and cut up clothes all over the floor. Harvey is laying motionless in the bed attached to tubes with his leg elevated in the air.

"An incision was made in his leg to relieve the pressure from the burns. In surgery, they'll remove all of the burned skin and place mesh skin grafts to encourage the growth of new skin. His jaw will probably not have to be wired, but he'll spend a few weeks on soft food. As for his pelvis—

"Stop, please." I say bluntly while staring at the man who broke my heart. As much as I want to be angry, the sight of him in this way is piercing my soul.

Denise moves closer to me.

"It hurts to see him like this." I admit.

"It's natural to be sad."

"Yeah, but he doesn't deserve it. Not from me."

"You'll have plenty of time to hate him. As for now, we have to pray he makes it through the surgery and recovers."

"Oh, he'll survive."

"Yes, faith is what we need."

"Yeah, naw, it's not faith. God doesn't want his ass right now and the devil isn't done using him." I wipe the few tears. "Where am I going to wait?" I turn and walk out leaving her standing there.

Once I get settled in the waiting room, I toll with calling Haven. It's almost four where she is. Sighing, I press her name.

"Mom," she groggily answers. "What's wrong?"

"I, um, your dad was involved in an accident."

"Is he okay?"

"No, but he will be. He was just taken to surgery to repair his pelvis, jaw and injuries to his right leg."

"Oh my God. Okay, I'm getting up to see about plane tickets. I'll let you know when I find something. Will you please keep me updated?"

"Of course. We'll talk soon."

Hanging up from her, I contemplate whether or not to call Harvey's sister, Haley. In the end, I decided she needs to know. After talking to her, she let me know she's not in a position to travel after having emergency surgery two days ago. I promised to keep her updated.

I sit back in the chair, closing my eyes to silently pray to God.

A few hours later, I jump when someone nudges me.

"Denise, is he okay?"

"Yes, come with me."

She takes me to a different area. Walking inside the room, Dr. Cartwright is talking to a nurse. When she leaves, he comes over to me.

"Mrs. Jennings, your husband's surgery was a success. We did what's called an internal pelvic fixation. It's where we reposition the displaced bones of his pelvis and hold them together with screws and metal plates. We removed the burned flesh from his leg. The great thing, he didn't have any bones exposed and the areas where the burns were deep, we covered with mesh that'll grow along with new skin. His jaw didn't have to be wired because we were able to relocate the bone, but he'll be on soft foods for at least three weeks. I will not lie, he's in for a long recovery which will require him to be immobile for a while, however he will survive. Do you have any questions for me?"

"How long will his hospital stay be, and can he be sent to a rehab?"

"We'll keep him here for up to a week and yes, that's an option."

"Great, then you've answered everything. Thank you."

"If you think of anything, let one of the nurses know and they can find me. Take care and I'll be back in the morning to check on him."

I walk to the end of his bed and stand there. The vibrating of my phone startles me. It's a Facetime from Haven.

"Hey," I whisper.

"How is he?"

I turn the phone for her to see and she gasps.

"It's worse than it looks, and the doctor says he'll be fine. You know your dad, he's strong and will be back to himself in no time."

"Thank God."

"What time does your plane land?"

"Four twenty-five."

"I'll be there to get you."

"Can you turn the phone back to daddy? Daddy, I love you, pull through and I'll be there soon."

Chapter 20

Later in the evening, I'm walking behind Haven into Harvey's room. When she abruptly stops, I bump into her.

"Haven, why did you stop in the doorway?" I look up to see Anette standing next to his bed wiping tears from her face as she stares at Harvey who is woke and unable to speak.

"Why isn't he saying anything?" she questions us.

"He has a dislocated jaw. Why are you here?" Haven asks.

Anette looks confused as Harvey releases her hand and reaches for Haven.

"Daddy, I'm here. Mom and I are here. Do you need anything?"

He shakes his head no. A few minutes later, the door opens with Dr. Cartwright and a nurse entering.

"Good evening. You two must be his daughters?" Dr. Cartwright asks.

"No, I'm his daughter and this is his friend."

"I'm his fiancé." Anette clarifies causing him to look over at me.

"Yep, everything you're thinking is probably right." I say.

He goes over to Harvey. "Mr. Jennings, I'm Dr. Cartwright."

"Doctor," Harvey whispers. "I'm Doctor Jennings."

He nods. "Dr. Jennings, I'm Dr. Cartwright, the attending physician overseeing your case."

"Can I see my file?" he gets out wiping his mouth where drool is pooling.

"Sir, I get you're a doctor, however, at this time you're my patient who needs to allow your jaw time to heal. Please stop talking. If you need to ask a question, write it down. I've had the nurse bring you this notepad and pen. As I was saying, I'm overseeing your care until you're discharged. You sustained some broken ribs and pelvis, along with third-degree burns on your legs. All of which were repaired during surgery. A bone in your jaw was dislocated and we were able to correct it, but you'll need to wear the bandage for a couple of weeks to ensure your jaw isn't opened wide enough to reinjury it."

Harvey rolls his eyes.

"Are you in any pain?"

He shakes his head no.

"Mrs. Jennings."

"Yes," Anette answers.

Dr. Cartwright looks at her then to me. "Mrs.," he emphasizes, "Jennings, do you have any questions?"

"No, I don't and thank you. And doctor, for the record, I'm only here because our divorce isn't final. You do, however, have my permission to relay any information to our daughter, Haven who will be his next of kin. Now, if dude wants you to talk to his girlfriend, have at it."

He glances at Harvey. "Sir, is this what you want?"

Instead of answering, he shuts his eyes and groans. I shake my head.

Dr. Cartwright smirks. "We can deal with all of this later. I'll have the nurse bring you something for pain and you should really try to rest. Mrs. Jennings, if there's anything you need or if something happens overnight, the nurses can reach me."

I nod and smile. When he leaves, I stand. "Haven, are you staying with your dad or coming home with me?"

"Staying."

Harvey opens his eyes. "Go home," he tells her. "I'll be okay."

"He'll be just fine because I'm here." Anette states rubbing his head.

"You aren't family." Haven clarifies.

"I'm as much family as you are."

"Says who? You're someone my dad had an affair with and produced a child, if it's even his. So, no sis, you aren't family."

"This is his son and we're getting married." She says louder. "You may not like me—

"We don't." Haven matter-of-factly states, cutting her off.

"That's your choice, but I'm not going anywhere."

"Stay or go, I don't care either way. It still won't make you family." She drops Harvey's hand and turns to me. "Mom, I changed my mind. I'm coming with you." Haven stomps to the elevator, stabbing the button with her finger. "She has some nerve."

"You do know she isn't the one to blame, right."

She looks at me bewildered. "You can't be serious. How can you even say that when she's a homewrecker."

The elevator opens, and I wait until we get inside.

"Mom?"

"The only way she could wreck our home, your dad had to give her access and permission. Haven, I didn't take vows with that girl, she isn't the one I created a home with nor did she make promises which were unkept. Your father did. She could only do what he allowed."

"So, you don't blame her?"

"I didn't say that. I said she isn't the one to blame, yet she still has fault because she's old enough to know right from wrong and I'm willing to bet she knew he was married. However, the majority of my anger is at him."

"Does this mean you're not going to help him through this?"

"That's exactly what it means."

Getting home, I sigh as Haven continues trying to convince me to be there for Harvey.

"Haven, I've heard all forty-five minutes of your reasoning as to why I should help your father, but my mind has not changed. I won't no part in taking care of him. He can go to rehab to get the care he needs until he's capable of taking care of himself."

"That can be months in a strange place."

"Obviously, strange places are what he likes and who am I to deny it."

"Mom, please. I promise to help with him."

"You can't promise that when your home is in California with your job."

"I can take some time off." She counters.

"No. He has Anette."

She boos.

"Like it or not, she's who he chose and apparently she's worth more than his family. With this being the case, there's no way I'm stopping my life to nurse him back to health only for him to leave again when he's well. No ma'am."

"You're still married though."

"And that means what? He wasn't thinking about our marriage when he slept with her without a condom to produce a child? He didn't give a damn about our marriage when he took his flat foot ass to a lawyer's office and had divorce papers drawn up? The same papers he delivered on my birthday after acting like everything was perfectly fine the night before. Now, I'm supposed to honor the vows and drop everything and wipe his ass? Girl bye."

"I'm sorry. I didn't mean to upset you."

"Well, you did. So, let me end this conversation for you. I ain't and I mean ain't. I ain't taking care of him, his broken pelvis, ribs, jaw or burns. I ain't visiting him in the hospital or sending well wishes and I ain't inviting him here. I also ain't wasting my prayers on him. If you want to give up your job and move back, go ahead but you might regret it."

"I can't leave him like this." She says getting emotional. "I'm sorry for expecting you to step in. He's not your responsibility anymore, I get it, but I can't go back to my life knowing he'll be stuck in some nursing home."

"You're grown. Make whatever decision that works for you. I'll only ask you to really think it through because the man who looks like your father isn't the one you've known your entire life."

"I'm going to bed."

"You aren't going to eat?" I ask referring to the Popeye's Chicken we picked up.

"I'm not hungry anymore. I'll see you in the morning."

"Suit yourself." I remove the food from the bag and as I think about the conversation, I start talking to myself. "I'm not going to be guilted into bringing him into this house. Dude left me for a girl half his age who probably doesn't know what it means to be a wife and now, I'm supposed to put my life on hold to nurse him back to health. I think not."

"I wasn't trying to guilt you."

I jump at the sound of Haven's voice. "I thought you were in your room."

"I was, but I forgot my phone. Mom, I apologize if I made it seem like I was guilting you. I guess I assumed because you're still married, he'd come home. I'm sorry. This is, I don't know, stuff happened so fast and I want to make sure he's getting the proper care."

"I understand, but it's not up to me anymore. When he walked out, he made it clear how he felt about me, his family and marriage and I will not forget it because he's in the hospital. Yes, it hurts to see him in this condition and if he couldn't make decisions on his own, I'd step in, but it's not the case. He chose someone else, let her take care of him."

She nods.

"Are you sure you don't want to eat something?"

She grabs a chicken leg and kisses me on the cheek. "Goodnight."

Chapter 21

A week later, I'm waken by knocking and the doorbell ringing. I pull on my robe, meeting Haven in the living room.

"What time is it?" she questions.

"Too early for whoever this is."

"Good morning, are you Won-um, how do you pronounce your name? Is it like Wanda, W-A-N-D-A? With these new spellings, I can never keep up."

"First off, who are you and why are you at my front door at the crack of dawn?"

"I'll call you Mrs. Jennings." She smiles, shrugging her shoulders. "Mrs. Jennings, my name is Carol Dillard and I work for Rest Assured Nursing. I'm here to ensure the room will be set up for your husband who will be coming home tomorrow."

"Carol Dillard, there must be a mistake. I don't have a husband, especially not one who's coming here."

"Oh yes dear. I have it right here on my paperwork. See. It says Mr. Harvey Jennings, this is your name as his wife and the address 5745 Wabash Cove, Memphis, TN 38125."

"I don't care what your paperwork says. Harvey doesn't live here anymore."

"Ma'am, I'm only following the orders given to me by Mr. Jennings. If now is a bad time, we can come back this afternoon."

"It won't be necessary." Harvey's attorney, David states walking up. "Wondah, unfortunately, Harvey's name is still on this house until the divorce is final, and he needs somewhere to rehab."

"Which is what rehabs are for. Better yet, why can't he go where he's been living seeing the divorce hearing is next week?"

"About that. One, he's living in a hotel. Not feasible for the quality of care he needs. Two, I petitioned to have the meeting set off until July 14th."

"You're a bold face lie if you think I'm putting up with him for that long. No, ain't no way. I'm calling my attorney."

"We can talk legal matters later. Right now, Harvey has chosen to come home which is his right."

"Dad, what's going on?" I hear Haven ask behind me. "Then why not talk to her? Mom was right. You're an asshole."

"Mrs. Jennings, can you show us where your husband will be staying?" Carol inquires.

"Sure. Follow me."

I turn and walk to the back door. "Here you are." Pointing outside.

"Wondah, come on." David says. "I know this is hard, but you're going to have to allow this. Show us where Harvey will be staying."

"Go to hell." I tell him. "You don't know anything about what's hard for me and you will not bring your Harry the Hippo looking ass in my house dictating shit."

"I'm not trying too. I only came to ensure things went smoothly."

"Smoothly? Y'all show up on my doorstep before the sun is fully up with this mess and think it's supposed to go smoothly. In what universe?"

"I know this isn't ideal, but by the time the divorce is final Harvey will be back on his feet and out of here."

"You're wrong. Whether he's on his feet or not, as soon as the divorce is decreed, you'll be picking his cripple ass up from the front lawn. Haven, show them to the guest room farthest from mine."

I go into my bedroom and slam the door. Grabbing my phone, I dial Nina's number.

"Wondah, is everything okay?"

"Why didn't you tell me the divorce hearing was set off for another month?"

"I found out late yesterday and planned to call you today. How did you find out?"

"Harvey's attorney delivered the news."

"What, when?"

"Just now. It seems my douche of an almost ex has decided to do his rehab here because technically the house still has his name on it."

She sighs. "I'm so sorry."

"It's cool."

"Wondah, please don't do anything to that man." She tells me.

"I wouldn't dare."

I hang up throwing the phone on the bed to hurriedly get dressed.

"Mom," Haven knocks. "The lady wants to know what to do with the bed they'll have to take down."

"It belonged to Harvey's mom. Tell her to throw it out."

"Where are you going?"

"To whoop your daddy."

Thirty-seven minutes exactly, I'm walking into Regional One and straight for dude's room. Barreling through the door, I don't even care it hits the wall. Pushing him in the chest, his eyes pop open. "How dare you. You treat me like scum of the earth and then expect to be allowed into the home you walked away from. And what? I'm supposed to just shut up, accept it and take care of you because you're hurt, and we're still married. Negro, they must have you on some very strong meds because your nuts aren't that big to try me like this."

"It's still mine." He says trying to keep from opening his mouth wide.

"Did you think about that before you signed it over to me in the divorce."

"Divorce isn't final."

"No, but we are, and you need to find somewhere else to stay."

He rolls his eyes. "Deal with it."

I grab him by the chin. His eyes get big as he tries to pry my hand loose.

"Come home." I challenge. "By all means, please come but I suggest you bring around the clock care because I'd hate for anything to happen to you."

"Ma'am, what are you doing?" A nurse asks.

"Talking to my husband." I squeeze harder. "See you tomorrow hun."

Making it home, I see Angelique's car. Getting inside, she's in the kitchen laughing with Haven and cooking breakfast. When they see me, Angel drops the fork and rushes over to the door.

"What are you doing?"

"Making sure the police aren't after you." She laughs.

"Whatever. I only went to talk and why are you here this early?"

"Haven called and well, I thought you could use the company and a good mimosa."

Haven's phone rings. "It's dad."

They both look at me.

Chapter 22

A few days later, I'm startled by the young man in my kitchen. "Who are you and why are you in my kitchen this late?" I ask pulling my robe closed.

"My name is Hasan, your husband's night nurse. Is there anything I can get you?"

"Um, no. Why are you in here?" I question.

"Getting your husband something to put on his stomach before he takes his medicine. He's awake if you'd like to sit with him."

"He's an almost ex and I'd rather sit in gas while lighting a cigarette. Now, when you're done making that sandwich, let him know he needs to furnish his own groceries or starve."

"Uh, yes ma'am."

I get a bottle of wine from the refrigerator, a corkscrew and head into my bedroom. Closing the door, I open the wine and sit it on the nightstand before grabbing my journal and pen and sitting in the middle of the bed.

June 16, 2020

11:57 PM

Today should have been the day I began my journey to freedom from the man I've spent most of my life with. A man I don't even know anymore. He looks the same, but everything about him is different. Yet, instead of celebrating my divorce, I've chosen to angrily drink. It's either drink or go across the hall to the guestroom and break the remaining ribs dude didn't crack in the accident.

Man!

Forgiveness is hard.

Forgiveness is hard to give.

Forgiveness is hard to give a person.

Forgiveness is hard to give a person who doesn't deserve it.

Man!

Good thing is, I've stopped questioning God because He wasn't answering anyway. Bad thing, now I'm questioning myself. How could I not know dude was unhappy? Was he unhappy? He had to be, right? Why else would he leave me for someone half his age. She's practically a child. What could she possibly give him, his wife couldn't that would make him walk away from everything? Was I that bad?

Was it the ten pounds I've gained or the gray hair in places women shouldn't have gray? Was he bored with me? Could I have stopped this?

I get angry and push the journal away. Reaching for the wine bottle, my iPad rings with a Facetime call from Denise. I hesitate to answer.

"What's up sis, something wrong? The last time you called, you had bad news about the cripple across the hall."

She laughs. "I felt the need to call. How are you?"

"You really want to know?"

"Of course."

"I feel like drinking this entire bottle of wine." I turn the camera to it and she exhales. "Am I being punished?"

"God doesn't work like that Wondah and you know it."

"There's things I thought I knew, but I was wrong and right now, this feels like punishment. Denise, how could he think coming here would be okay? He initiated a divorce, giving up rights to everything and walked away without a conversation or explanation. If this isn't bad enough, he treats me like I'm the one to blame. Then he has the nerve to waltz his burnt ass in here, well be pushed in a wheelchair, like I should be okay with it talking about it's still his house. It's also still within my right to kick his ass but I ain't done it." I blabber.

"Well, technically you have kicked his butt. Twice, I think but why the man got to be burnt?"

I chuckle. "He is." Sighing, I release tears. "Why did I deserve this? Did I do something wrong? Was

I such a bad wife that after twenty-seven years, he could discard me and look at me with eyes which seems as though his heart never loved me? Was I simply a place filler until he got tired?" I cry. "Did I deserve this?"

"Wondah, nobody deserves pain, disrespect and unfaithfulness and you didn't do anything. This is on Harvey." She tells me.

"He isn't the one suffering though." I sniffle. "He gets to walk away unaffected while I'm left broken, questioning my womanhood and sanity. I'm looking at myself in the mirror and seeing a failure because a man I've loved for over thirty years left me for a child half his age. What could she possibly have or do, I couldn't?" I sob. "Then, when I was about to close the door on the situation and heal, here he comes to kick it wide open again. I hate him. I hate him. I hate him. I'm not supposed to, but I hate him for what he did and for what it's turning me into. God!"

"Wondah, listen to me. Harvey's choosing of that little girl says absolutely nothing about you and everything about him. You're a doggone great woman and I'll not sit by while you think anything less. He messed up, not you and you won't take the blame for his actions. Not on my watch. Sister, I don't know how God is going to use you through this, but I need you to trust Him. I don't know how God is going to use this situation to restore you, but I need you to trust Him."

"I'm trying. I've been calling, and He hasn't showed up yet."

"What if He doesn't? In Second Corinthians, twelve and nine, Paul said he begged God three times to remove his thorn. A thorn which was causing him pain and agony. A thorn Paul describes as being a messenger of Satan given to torment him. Although Paul's thorn was to keep him from being conceited, what if Harvey is your thorn to trust God's ability to be your strength in weakness."

"Seriously, I hear you and I trust God but—

"There is no but after I trust God. It's I trust God, period. Sister, nobody but God and Harvey know why this happened the way it did, and you've got to stop trying to figure it out. Tell God, you trust Him and whatever His will is. Do you know what God told Paul, in response to his ask of removing the thorn?"

"He told him, My grace is sufficient." I answer.

"Yes, sufficient meaning to defend and ward off. Sis, you got everything you need to survive this, even with your thorn being across the hall."

"I believe you, but sometimes this thorn feels like it's piercing my lungs making it hard to breathe."

"During those times, call me and I'll be your oxygen."

"I know you will, but you have your own family and it's not fair for me to need you more than your husband."

"He understands."

"He may, but it's not right and I thank you for offering. I'm going to get through this."

"Whenever you need me, I'm here. Until then I'll send you a playlist I created. Listen to the song by Earnest Pugh called "I Trust You.""

I nod.

"I love you and put the cork back in the wine."

"I will after a few sips. Love you, bye."

Ending the call, I push the journal and iPad away. After my promised sips, I turn out the light and slide under the covers. A few seconds pass before the text message notification sounds. I click on the playlist searching for the song. Pressing play, I lay the phone on my chest and close my eyes.

"I trust you Lord. I trust you Lord. Whatever your will is Lord, I trust you." The song plays.

Chapter 23

Walking out of my bedroom, I almost bump into a young lady who is helping Harvey down the hall. His eyes snap up at me.

"My apologies ma'am." She says. "We're almost done."

I nod at her, roll my eyes at him and move pass them. Turning into the kitchen, Haven is sitting at the table with her computer and headphones in.

"Yes sir, thank you. I'll be back in the office on Monday. I appreciate it. See you then. Good morning." She says after closing her laptop.

"You're leaving?"

"Yes, I have a big project that was assigned to me. You don't mind, do you?"

"Of course not." I tell her grabbing my travel mug from the cabinet and filling it with coffee.

"Are you and dad going to be okay?"

"I don't have a problem with her." Harvey says walking with the physical therapist into the kitchen.

"Her has a name asshole. And yes, we will be fine as long as he stays away from me."

"Haven, will you fix me a cup of coffee?" he asks ignoring me.

I take the pot and pour it down the drain.

"Mom."

"Whoops." I grab my things and head out, passing Isabel on the way in.

"Good morning Mrs. Wondah. Is there anything you need me to do today besides the usual?"

"Nope and don't let Harvey overwork you. This is my home. Utilize your normal schedule and let his folk take care of him. If he or they add anything extra, make him pay for it."

"Yes ma'am."

Walking into the office, Asha is behind me to go over the schedule for the day.

"Good morning boss lady. How are things at the O.K. Corral aka your house?"

"Girl, I don't have words to describe it other than to say, a mess." I shake my head. "Anyway, what's on the agenda today?"

"You have new clients coming in. Mr. and Mrs. Lincoln and Teah, spelled T-E-A-H Harris. Here are the forms they filled out. Short version, they've been married for seventeen years, two children, she's a principal and he own Harris Heating and Air."

"What's their chief complaint?"

"They don't have one."

"Come again."

"Mrs. Harris said she saw on your website where a marriage needs a tune-up, every now and then and she feels with their youngest getting ready to go off to college, this is the perfect time to ensure they are still what each other needs."

"Sounds good. What time will they be here?"

"Eleven forty-five."

"Thanks."

When she leaves, I get a call from Pastor Brielle.

"Pastor Brielle, how are you?" I answer.

"Good morning Wondah, I'm great and I want to start by apologizing for just now reaching out. First, how are you?"

"I'm taking it as it comes." I smile hoping it carries over to my tone.

"Taking it as it comes may prove to be harder and heavier than you can bear. Instead, you have to take what you can handle. Wondah, I won't beat around the bush. I had a meeting with Harvey after being made aware of things in his personal life and he told me about the divorce. When there's sudden change in one's life, the enemy will use that to destroy the very foundation of your faith. I will not lie and say I know how it feels to be in your storm, but the church and I are here for you and we've been praying. Is there anything else we can do for you?"

"Pray harder." I chuckle trying not to get emotional. "It's hard and sometimes I feel as though my prayers are in vain. The more I cry out to God, the farther from Him I feel." I admit. "Is He ever going to show up?"

"In John eleven, Martha felt like you. She was angry at Jesus for not showing up when they called Him while in agony and pain. While they watched their brother suffer in sickness, they called the one person they knew could help Him and He didn't come when they expected Him too. In anger, she and Mary both told him, "if You'd been here, my brother wouldn't have died." Sometimes, we feel as though God has to show up for us immediately. What if He doesn't? He can still work, and His power is everlasting no matter when He comes. In this case, Jesus waited in order for the people to know it wasn't medicine that saved Lazarus, it was Him. Sister Wondah, I have to believe God will show up for you too. When He does, you nor your degree and knowledge in marriage counseling will be able to take the credit for getting you through. It'll be all God."

"Pastor Brielle," I pause taking breaths trying to stop the shakiness in my voice. "I don't understand how we ended up here."

"Would knowing how make the difference? Would it make the pain any less? Would it help you sleep at night?"

"Maybe not."

"Have you ever seen a person who's been stabbed ask the one inflicting the pain how they held the knife? The how isn't important, the healing is. Wondah, this is the time you have to heal. If not, you run the risk of this pain becoming an infection that can kill you. Yes, it hurts, and healing seems to be slow, but let patience have her perfect work that you may be perfect and entire, wanting nothing. Can I pray for you?" she asks.

"Yes ma'am."

"Dear Heavenly Father, your word tells us in Psalm 118 and five when we're hard pressed to call You, You'll answer and set us in a broad place. A secure place for us to heal and surrender in peace. Well Father, as your humble servant, I come seeking that place for my sister Wondah who suddenly found herself in a storm when the wind picked up, rain started to pour, and darkness settled before she had time to react. Suddenly, her life shifted, leaving her off balance and confused.

And now God, we call out to you asking for her to be clothed with strength to stand when the enemy is beckoning for her to give up. Give her patience when it seems like healing is happening in slow motion. Protect her when she feels as though she's surrounded by evil and temptations. Restore her so she doesn't forsake love again and redeem whatever time she thinks she's lost." She speaks in tongue.

"Father, she may not understand, she may shed tears, she may lash out and may even want to turn away from everything and everybody she's known and it's okay. Just let her survive it, stronger and wiser. And when her storm is over, You ensure her identity is of a woman who will boldly, unapologetically, willingly and faithfully know exactly who she is. Divorce may have tried to take who she was, but it cannot touch who she's always been destined to be. So, we thank you storm for cleaning away what we didn't even realize we no longer needed. Thank you storm for testing our strength and our sanity. It looked bad there for a minute and she almost gave up, but now she has her second wind to try again. Lord, we thank you and we trust you. Amen."

"Amen. Lord, I thank you. Pastor Brielle, I love you and I'm grateful for you taking the time to pour into me."

"I love you too and I'm always here. Take care and I'll see you Sunday."

I get up from my desk and begin to walk in circles, thanking God.

"Father, I trust you and I need you. Come into my life and handle whatever task, enemy and evil I can't see or defeat. Don't allow me to lose myself in this storm. It happened, I can't change it, but I sure can survive it. Amen."

I spend a few more minutes in prayer before going into the bathroom to get myself together.

Chapter 24

"Good morning. You must be Teah?"

"Yes, and this is my husband Lincoln." She says taking my hand.

"Please have a seat and tell me why you came to see me today."

"Well," she looks at her husband, "I don't think my husband is satisfied with me anymore."

He sits up and turns to her. "Why would you think that? You told me we were coming here for a tune up, whatever that is."

"You barely touch me anymore. There used to be a time I couldn't pass you without you grabbing a part of me. Now, it's get up in the morning, get dressed, go to work, come home, dinner, shower, tv and bed. Oh, sprinkle in Tamara's soccer games and whatever else. Rinse and repeat."

"If I may ask, when was the last time you've been intimate?" I inquire and they both look at each other. "I mean the real kind of intimacy that has you sore in all the right places, smiling at each other like giddy teenagers and makes you remember why you've made it seventeen years."

"Too long." They say together.

"Even when I initiate it, he's too tired to give me his full attention."

"This is why it's important for your marriage to have tune ups, every once in a while. With a car, a tune-up is essential to maintaining your car's performance and longevity by checking and replacing worn out and damaged engine parts. In a marriage, it serves the same purpose. You two are the engine, serving in different capacities to ensure your marriage last. Over time, things can run smoothly, or you can get comfortable forgetting to get the scheduled maintenance, only to be reminded by the check engine light. At that point, it's usually a problem which can cost a lot to repair or worst-case scenario, the engine locks up. I want each of you to stand and put your backs together."

I wait until they do.

"Mr. Harris, describe what your wife has on."

"Uh," he scratches his head. "She has on a pair of jeans, shirt and sandals."

"What about her hair?"

"Braids, I think."

"Mrs. Harris, what is your husband wearing?"

"Levi jeans, a company t-shirt, worn out pair of Nike tennis shoes, a low haircut and his company hat. I know because it's all he ever wears."

"You both can sit. I did this to see if you notice each other because whether you realize it or not, when you stop paying attention is when you miss the signs. The signs indicating there's something wrong in the engine and if it's not dealt with soon—

"The engine locks up." Mr. Harris finishes.

"Mr. Harris, is your marriage over?"

"No. God no. I love this woman with every fiber of my being. I wouldn't know how to function tomorrow if I woke up and she wasn't there. And this has nothing to do with how she keeps the house. When we met, I was broken from a failed relationship and mommy issues. I didn't think I've ever be good enough for somebody's husband. Then this lady walked into the company I worked, and my spirit leaped.

On our first date, I told her everything about me and she didn't run. Instead, she invited me to church." He chuckles. "She said, she didn't have a right to judge my past, but if I was her future, I needed to be healed. Dr. Jennings, this woman would lay on her face in my living room praying for me when I didn't even desire a relationship with God. It's because of her I received favor from God. I owe her."

"Linc, you don't owe me, and I don't want you to want me because you think you do." She tells him frustrated.

"Teah, I don't want you, I need you. My breathing isn't the same without your aroma and my taste isn't the same without the season your touch gives. Baby, I'm sorry I've allowed too much time to pass without showing how much you mean to me. I apologize for missing the warning signs, but I'll be damned if I let this engine lock up."

"Teah, tell your husband what you need."

She turns to him. "I need you to keep being the head of our house and I also need your hands to touch me, your heart to love me, your lips to kiss me, your eyes to see me, your soldier to infiltrate my battlefield and for us to continue making memories."

I smile. "Mr. Harris, what do you need from your wife?"

"I need her to give me another chance."

"You have it."

"I also need her to take my hand and allow me to lead her to the car, so I can get a room at the Hilton across the street because we're not going to make it home."

She laughs.

"I'm so serious." He tells her.

I scribble something on a piece of paper and stand. "The hardest part was coming here. Everything else is up to you two. Here."

"A prescription?" Teah says.

"For a tune-up."

He grabs her hand, pulling her out the door.

I'm laughing when Asha comes in with a confused look on her face.

"Don't even ask."

Chapter 25

I walk into the house to see Harvey and Haven sitting in the living room. They're both asleep on the couch. I stand at the door remembering when I used to love to see this. Now, it makes my skin burn with anger. I go into the kitchen and slam a cabinet. Then I slam the refrigerator and the door to the pantry.

"Hey." Haven says walking in. "You okay?"

"Oh, I'm just great. Blessed and highly favored of the Lord. What about you?"

She sits at the island. "We were watching a movie."

I take a deep breath. "I'm sorry." I tell her. "Seeing him here like it used to be aggravates the hair on my big toe."

"Ma," she laughs.

"I'm so serious. Who's is this?" I ask about the food on the stove.

"Yours. I got your favorite from the Chop Suey House."

"Thanks."

"Dad had a doctor's appointment today."

"Did they discuss when he'll be out of here?" I ask.

"Ma, I know this situation isn't ideal, but is it really that bad?"

"Nope, it's worse."

She sighs. "His jaw is better, and he no longer needs to wear the bandage. His pelvis is getting stronger, but he'll need a few more weeks of physical therapy before he can retire the walker."

"Haven, baby, it's great he's getting better. I'm happy because it gets him out of here, but I don't need details. Has he heard from Haley?"

"Yes, she called earlier. She had to have her appendix removed, but hopes she'll be able to fly here in a few weeks."

"Good. Maybe she'll take him back to South Carolina." I smirk.

She turns to leave then stops. "Can we have dinner here tomorrow since I leave Saturday?"

"If you mean we," I say pointing between the two of us, "then yeah."

"I meant you, me, Angelique, Auntie Nise, Uncle Daniel, Sharda, Chad and daddy."

"Haven, I love you and would give up a kidney to save your life, but I ain't eating nothing with dude."

"Ma, he'll be in the guestroom."

"You're right. His ass will be in the guestroom because I'm not eating with him and I mean it."

"Ma."

"Leave it alone Haven."

"Fine. Don't worry about it."

I come out of my bathroom and see Haven reading my journal. I walk over and snatch it from her. "What are you doing?"

"I didn't know it was your journal, at first. I was looking for something and saw it."

"And instead of you minding your business, you opened it. You had no right. This is personal."

"Are you suicidal?"

I exhale.

"Are you?"

"No."

"Then why did you write it?" she asks.

"Because that's what a journal is for, to write your feelings. Was I suicidal? No, but when you're going through pain, a lot of things cross your mind you don't normally think about. For me, at this particular time, it was suicide. Not the action, just a thought. It was in that moment, I understood the mind of someone who's been there."

"I'm sorry."

"For what?"

"For not understanding what you're going through." She tells me.

"You're not supposed to, and I pray you'll never experience this. Haven, sixty-nine days ago, life changed, and I didn't have a say in the matter. It changed abruptly leaving me distraught because I couldn't fix it. During most of those nights, I was either drinking, staring at the ceiling or stalking dude's Facebook page. There were hours I didn't think I'd make it and some of those times, I didn't want too. Everything was hurting, yet I was never at a place of actually committing or contemplating suicide. However, I now understand a person who has. Just maybe God will use this to strengthen my sanity to help somebody else."

I wipe the tears streaming down her face.

"I'm going to be okay." I assure her.

"How can you be sure?"

"I have no other choice."

She hugs me and once she's gone, I grab my journal and pen.

June 18, 2020

Sometimes the storm isn't because you're being punished, it could be because you told God yes.

"Thank you, Holy Spirit." I say out loud.

I realized this while talking to my daughter. See, on my birthday I prayed and told God to guide, fill and lead me in the direction of my life's assignment even if I had to disconnect from what I'm comfortable with. Only to get up, the same morning and be handed divorce papers. Here I thought God was punishing me when He was doing what I asked.

I drop the pen and fall down on my knees.

"Dear God, please accept my apology. I've been mad at you when it's been me the entire time. Forgive me because I'm ready now. Holy Spirit help me make up the time I've lost to anger, bitterness and resentment. Help me to get out of the way in order to see all you have for me. Open doors predestined and close doors hindering. Father, I trust you. It may have taken me sixty-nine days, but I'm here now and I'm ready. Amen."

I grab my phone to play Denise's playlist and for the first time, in sixty-nine days, I'm looking forward to going to sleep.

Chapter 26

Walking into Stoney River, the young lady is showing me to the bar when a distracted server causes me to bump into a gentleman already sitting causing him to spill his drink.

"Oh God, I'm so sorry. I'll replace your drink."

When he turns around, I step back. "Dr. Cartwright?"

"Mrs. Jennings. Please call me Alonzo."

"And please call me Wondah. I apologize for bumping into you. I was trying not to get ran over by the server."

"It's not a problem. If I'm going to be bumped into, I'd rather it be a woman who look as amazing as you."

I smile.

"Ma'am, would you still like the seat at the end of the bar?" the hostess asks.

"She can have this one."

I nod to her and she walks off.

"How's your husband?" he inquires motioning for the bartender.

"He's an almost ex who's still alive, so I'd say he's doing okay."

"That bad, huh?"

"Worse."

He laughs before holding up his glass to signal for another drink.

"What would you like to drink?" he questions when the bartender stops in front of us.

"A strawberry Hennessy, please."

The bartender nods and walks away.

"Tell me, Alonzo, what are you doing sitting at a bar alone on a Sunday afternoon."

"It's the first time I've been off in fourteen days and since I overslept and missed church, I decided to stop in and get lunch. What about you?"

"I was headed home from church and didn't feel like cooking a meal for one, so here I am."

"It takes getting used to, doesn't it?"

I take a sip from the glass the bartender sits in front of me and give him the thumbs up.

"Would you like to order something to eat?"

"Yes, the ahi tuna salad and a glass of water."

When he leaves, I look at Alonzo, confused by his question. "What do you mean?"

"Being a party of one. It's been almost two years for me and some days, I still have to remind myself of it."

"Divorce?"

He nods.

"I'm sorry to hear that."

"It was for the best because we both had different expectations of marriage even after ten years."

"Why did it take ten years to figure it out?"

"We knew early on, but complacency and comfort will keep you in places you've outgrown."

"Until she met somebody." I say.

"How'd you know?"

"I'm a marriage counselor by day. And to answer your earlier question, yes, it takes a lot of getting used too. Dude and I were together thirty years and when you're accustomed to doing things a certain way, it takes a lot of time to forget it. How are you handling the divorce? If it's too personal, you don't have to answer."

"I keep busy."

"In other words, you aren't."

"No, maybe not." He laughs. "Honestly, I didn't think it would affect me, as much as it has, seeing she and I were already living together separately."

"Living together separately, that's a new one."

"We were living together in separate bedrooms, she had her life and I had mine. When she finally admitted to meeting someone and wanting the divorce, I didn't hesitate. Then I came home and the first two nights, I was okay. The third and fourth nights made it real. She wasn't singing in the kitchen or stretched out across the couch with the TV's volume on one hundred. Don't misunderstand me, our marriage was over, but I'd gotten use to our routine and when it ended, it left a void."

A server sits my salad in front of me and while Alonzo orders another drink, I bow to say grace.

"What about you? How are you handling your divorce?" he asks me.

"I have to get divorce first." I put a fork of salad in my mouth and he waits. "Our hearing was pushed back because of the accident and dude used that legality as a means of moving back in."

"Ouch."

"Yeah, and seeing him and I aren't amicable, it's been rough."

"I can't say I'm shocked. The few days I attended to him, let's just say he wasn't the best patient or man."

"A few months ago, I'd argue to say you're wrong. However, I don't know the man he's become."

"Maybe something happened to him or he's having a midlife crisis."

"Well, it's not up to me to figure it out. All I know is, fingers crossed, our hearing will happen in three weeks and I can finally be free of him."

His phone vibrates. He looks at it and shakes his head.

"Work." He motions for the bartender and hands him his card. "Can you close out both of our checks."

"You don't have to cover my tab."

"Take it as appreciation for spending your Sunday afternoon with me."

He signs the receipt and slides his card into his wallet. "Wondah, if it's not too soon, I'd love to take you out for a celebratory drink once your divorce is final."

I lay my fork down and wipe my mouth with the napkin before getting my phone. Unlocking it, I hand it to him to enter his number. He presses it to call my phone.

"I'd like that. Thank you for lunch and I look forward to that drink."

Walking into the house, I roll my eyes when Harvey is sitting in the living room with his attorney.

"Good afternoon Wondah." David stands.

"I hope on baby Jesus you're not here to say anything about the hearing being changed." I tell him.

"No, no. I'm meeting with Harvey about something else."

"Great."

"Wait. I know this is a far-fetched request, but is it possible for Harvey to remain here for another fourteen days after the hearing?"

"Let's see. He's been here for thirteen days already with the intent on staying another twenty-three until our court date. The entire time he's been here, he hasn't opened his mouth to say two words to me. Yet, he eats my food, uses my good electricity, hot water, towels and WIFI, he doesn't pay for anymore and now, you want me to let him stay an additional fourteen. Hell no. Y'all must be on some good drugs to keep thinking this type of crap will fly."

"His physical therapist says he should be good on his own by then and his house will be ready."

"How do you know he won't be ready before then?"

"We don't."

"Right. So, tell your mute client the answer is still no."

"Wondah, please. I can ask the judge, but I'd rather not have her make this an order because then she can give up to thirty days. Please. Fourteen days is all I'm asking."

"I'll take my chances with the judge."

Chapter 27

Friday night, I get home from a session at Release and picking up a pizza from Coletta's. Sitting it on the stove, I go into my bedroom to shower. Once done, I put on pajama shorts and tank top. Walking back down the hall, I hear something fall in the guestroom where Harvey is staying.

I keep walking.

In the kitchen, I wash my hands, grab a paper plate from the pantry and prepare to eat dinner.

I hear loud moaning.

I get a bottle of tea from the refrigerator, place two slices of pizza on my plate and get ready to walk into the living room.

"Wondah."

"No, this black, cripple piece of crap didn't call my name." I put everything down and break a piece of the pizza. Getting to the door of the guestroom, I push it open to find him slumped on the side of the bed, forehead covered in sweat with one foot in his pajama pants.

"What?" I ask taking a bite of the pizza and leaning against the door frame.

"I wouldn't ask if I didn't need it, but could you please help me."

I chew slowly before swallowing. "Help you with what exactly?"

He winces in pain. "Putting on my pants."

I put the last of the pizza into my mouth and slowly lick my fingers.

"Please." He repeats.

"Naw dude, where your peoples at?"

"Wondah, please. Hasan had an emergency and the lady covering for him is having car trouble."

"You don't have life alert?"

"Will you please help me?" he asks breathing hard. "I know I'm the last person who should be asking you anything, however I really need you."

"You really need me? You didn't think I really needed my husband? You didn't think I really needed to know my husband was having an affair with a little girl? You didn't think I really needed a heads up on your plans to divorce me?"

"I'm sorry." He groans. "I'm sorry for everything."

"You're a liar. You're only sorry because you really need me."

I turn to walk out, and he yelps in pain.

I stop and close my eyes. Biting my bottom lip and balling my hands into fist, I want to put my right foot in front of the left to get back to my pizza.

"Wondah, please."

"Fine."

I turn back, snatching his leg and putting it into his pants. Placing the walker in front of him, he moans while positioning himself to stand. When he does, I bend over to pull them up. Raising up, he's glaring at my chest where my tank has come down. I don't bother to fix it.

"Um hello, can you slide your ass in the bed because my dinner is getting cold."

"You smell good." He tells me.

"I taste even better. Oh, my bad. You don't get the luxury of that anymore."

I leave him standing there and head back into the kitchen. A few minutes later, I hear him coming down the hall. He stops at the door of the living room.

"Thank you." He says.

I turn the volume up on the surround sound.

Fifteen minutes later, I go to get more pizza. Dude is sitting at the counter looking lost.

"Did you forget why you're in here?" I ask.

"Do you mind if I get a slice of pizza?"

Shaking my head, I get another slice and throw him the box.

"Can you—

"No, I can't do nothing else for you. Either call 911 or Jesus."

"Wondah, I know I hurt you and I've gone about things the wrong way, but I truly am sorry."

"I believe that as much as I believe in aliens. If you were sorry, you wouldn't have handled things the way you did. If you were truly sorry, you would have been honest with your wife of twenty-seven years. Instead, you allowed your penis to do the thinking by impregnating a girl who's a few years older than your daughter."

"She lied about her age."

"And you've lied about everything else afterwards. Y'all deserve each other."

"Will you give me a minute to explain."

"Dude, there's nothing you can say to me and no apology big enough for me to ever trust, respect or believe in you again. You chose your new life and after the divorce, treat me as if I never existed."

"Isn't that being extreme when we do have a daughter together?"

"She's grown and doesn't need us to co-parent."

"What about holidays, weddings and the birth of her children?"

"Do you hear yourself? You must have a tumor the doctors didn't find during the accident because it's the only thing that can count for this level of stupidity spewing from your mouth. You've been in my house for weeks and barely mumbled three words and now because I helped pull your pants up, it has changed your heart posture towards me. Wow. All it took was bending down to slide your leg into some pajama pants for you to be concerned about the state of our relationship going forward. Had I known, I'd left your cripple ass leaning against the bed until morning. From now on, make sure the people you hired to take care of you are here because I won't be doing this again."

Chapter 28

Three Weeks Later

Tuesday morning, I meet my attorney, Nina King in front of the courtroom.

"Wondah, as we discussed last night, this is the formal hearing where the judge will ask questions to ensure everything is still in agreement. All you have to do is answer."

"Once this is done, can she finalize everything, or will I have to wait?"

"It's totally up to her. She can sign the decree today or it'll be a few days."

"Dude's attorney said he can ask the judge to allow him to stay in the house another thirty days, is this true?"

"Unfortunately, because the house is still in both names, she can. However, again, strange things have happened. If it seems like she's leaning in that direction, we can always counter."

"Please do. The sooner he's out of my space and face, the better."

"No problem. I'll see you inside."

I turn in time to see Harvey walking in on a cane. He doesn't look in my direction and that's perfectly fine with me. Since the conversation a few weeks ago, he hasn't said anything to me, but he made sure his caretakers were there.

Inside the courtroom, we are sworn in after Judge Cynthia Chavis is seated.

"Good morning ladies and gentlemen. This is the case of Harvey Jennings versus Wondah Jennings. Is this right?"

"Yes, your honor."

"Very well. I'll ask both parties to please state your names for the record."

"Harvey Jennings."

"Wondah Jennings."

"Were you both residents of Tennessee for six months, immediately before you filed for divorce?"

"Yes," we state.

"Has there been a Marital Dissolution Agreement entered into by both parties that fairly and equitably divides all assets and debts?"

"Yes, your honor. My client has removed his name from the practice belonging to Mrs. Jennings, they've handled the financial accounts amicably and his name will be removed from the house at the final decree of divorce." David states.

"Very well. Mrs. Jennings, do you have any objection?"

"About the house. Dude, I mean Mr. Jennings moved himself back in after an accident. How long am I obligated to let him stay?"

"Until the divorce is final, and his name is removed."

"We actually no longer need him to stay. Mr. Jennings will be moving out of the marital home on tomorrow." David corrects

"Hallelujah. Your honor. I have no objection."

"Do you share any biological children?" she inquires.

"Yes, your honor. Their daughter Haven is twenty-three."

"What about continuing health insurance coverage?" Judge Chavis questions flipping through papers.

"It's on page twelve of the agreement, your honor." Nina states. "Both parties will cover their own medical and life insurance plans."

"As part of your agreement, will you each be covering your own court costs?"

"No, your honor. Mr. Jennings is covering all costs." Nina asserts. "As per the agreement."

"And are you asking the court to grant a divorce on the ground of irreconcilable differences?"

"Yes, your honor."

"Are there any other details we need to cover or any last-minute changes preventing this divorce from being decreed on today?"

"No, your honor."

"Then it shall be ordered according to the Marital Dissolution Agreement before me, it is agreed as follows. There will be no spousal support paid by either of you nor a splitting of assets from Mr. Jennings 401k plan. Mrs. Jennings will retain the marital home, the business located at 7890 Rushing Avenue called Begin Again, the 2020 Cadillac XT6, all finances in joint bank accounts and her own health, life and auto insurance. Is this the final and agreed upon dissolution of marriage?" she asks looking at both of us.

"That's correct," I say wiping tears.

"That's correct." Harvey adds.

"Then it is so ordered, and I hereby enter the official judgment of resolution on this 14th day of

July in the year two thousand and twenty. I usually wait to go through the divorce agreements again before signing, but all seems to be in order and there's no need for me to wait." The judge hits the gavel and I jump.

"Are you okay?" Nina questions.

"It only took twenty minutes to dissolve thirty years. Is this all?" I ask her.

"There's one more form to fill out called the Dissolution of Marriage Judgment and then you are officially divorced. You'll be able to get a certified copy of the agreement in a few days."

"What are the next steps to have him removed from the house's deed?"

"Get a copy of the deed, fill out and file what's called a Quit Claim Deed at the local Register of Deeds office which may have a small fee attached and it'll be removed. It's a simple process. If you need my assistance, you know where to find me."

"Thanks Nina."

Walking to the elevator, I press the button and after a few seconds it opens. Getting inside, my phone dings with a text from Alonzo. A smile grows across my face until David puts his hand in to stop the doors from closing. I roll my eyes before stepping back.

"Wondah, congratulations on the divorce."

I raise my head and glare at him.

"I thought you'd be happy to get Harvey out of your house."

"David, what do you want?"

"Seeing I'm no longer your husband's attorney, well for the divorce, how about I take you out for a celebratory drink?"

"I'd rather drink the saliva of a baby alligator."

"You don't mean that, and Harvey never has to know."

"I wouldn't care if it was broadcasted on a Blip billboard, my answer is still no and the audacity of you to even ask fifteen seconds after my divorce is final. You're pitiful and I pray no woman ever falls victim to you."

The doors open, and I mug him walking out.

Chapter 29

Later that evening, after stopping to get my locs retwisted, I'm home getting dressed to meet Alonzo for drinks at Season's 52 when the doorbell rings. Opening it, I'm met with a large assortment of balloons.

"Hello."

Snatching them out the way, I laugh at Denise, Angelique and Sharda standing there with party hats, rattles and confetti. Denise pulls me onto the porch, pointing to the yard.

"What did y'all do?" I rush down the steps to see the yard sign *Happily Divorced* displayed in big letters. "Oh my God." I laugh.

"Uh, wait one minute. You're not dressed for a night in. Where are you going?" Angelique asks with her arms folded.

"Out for drinks."

"Out for drinks with who?"

"Who says I'm going out with anybody? Can't a grown woman celebrate her divorce without needing company?" I smirk while moving in between them to go back into the house.

"Oh no heifer. You better spill it. Ain't no way in God's wonderful creation of Heaven and Earth are you going out by yourself smelling this good. What is this I smell?" Denise sniffs me. "Is that," she sniffs, "magic body frosting from Bubble Bistro?"

"And," Sharda sniffs, "ginger peach plus pretty lady with a little bit of loopy body oil?"

"Will y'all stop?" I laugh as they follow me into my bedroom.

"With the fresh twists and updo. Aw snap and she's wearing heels. Yasss, I'm here for it, Ms. Wondah Renee Parker."

"Hey Ms. Parker," they all sing.

"Okay, okay. I'm going to have drinks with a guy. His name is Alonzo Cartwright."

"Gul, shut your mouth and keep on talking." Denise squeals. "The Dr. Alonzo Cartwright from Regional One Medical who happened to have taken care of your husband after his accident."

"Ex-husband and yes."

"Well dang sis." Angelique smiles.

"We're only friends. He asked to take me out for a celebratory drink and I agreed." I tell them while putting on my jeans.

"How would he know there was something to celebrate?" Sharda questions.

"I told him when we had lunch a few weeks back."

"Lunch?" they all scream.

"Good Lord. I bumped into him at Stoney River after church one Sunday. We exchanged numbers and a few texts here and there. He asked if he could take me out for drinks and I agreed. Y'all are making this into something bigger than it is." I tell them while sliding on a white one shoulder top.

"Says the one with her entire left shoulder out."

"That's it, I'm not going."

"We're only kidding. Stop being dramatic."

I slump on the bed. "Am I being foolish to be going out with someone on the same day of my divorce hearing?"

"Uh hello. Your ex has a whole teenager pregnant and you're worried about going out for drinks with a friend. Girl bye. If anybody wants to judge you, send them to me so I can tell them to judge they mammy." Sharda states.

"Wondah, go out and enjoy yourself. You deserve it."

I slip on my sandals and stand.

"You look beautiful."

"You look happy."

"You look blessed."

They all look at each other before running up and hugging me.

Half hour later, after letting the ladies convince me into a mini photo shoot, I walk out the house to Harvey getting out of his car. He stops to stare at me and I do a full turn for him to see every inch. Smiling I get into my truck and pull out.

Making it to the restaurant, I take a deep breath and step inside to look for Alonzo.

"Wow."

I turn to see him smiling.

"You look stunning." He says walking closer to kiss me on the cheek.

"Thank you."

"Sir, your table is ready."

He holds out his hand for me, leading me to the table. We take our seats as the hostess explains the specials for the night.

"I hope this doesn't sound weird, but divorce looks great on you."

"Thank you."

The server takes our order for drinks and an appetizer of crab cakes.

"How do you feel now the divorce is done?" he inquires.

"To be honest, it hasn't fully hit me yet. However, I'm grateful it's over. I have a few more loose ends to tie up and then I'm looking forward to next."

Our drinks are delivered. Alonzo picks up his glass. "To closed doors, new beginnings and next."

"Amen."

Over dinner I learn more about Alonzo. He's 51, divorced, no children, surgeon, follower of God and loves to read, travel and work in the yard. His mom, grandmother and younger brother live in Arlington, TN although he doesn't get to spend a lot of time with them due to his hectic work schedule. Me, I give him a quick recap of my life. Recently turned 50, one daughter, licensed marriage therapist with a PhD in Counseling Psychology who loves a great cigar, glass of bourbon and music. I tell him about our church and invite him to service one Sunday.

"Thank you for a wonderful evening. I have to admit I was nervous coming here." I tell him once the server is done clearing the table.

"So was I." He chuckles. "It's been a while since I've had dinner across from a beautiful woman."

"Really, why?"

"After Vivian, I threw myself into work. I didn't want my next relationship to be because of loneliness or a rebound before I've had time to heal and decide if another marriage is what I desire."

"That's very adult of you. You don't know the many couples I've had to counsel through hard times for this very reason. Most don't understand the pull flesh has over our decision making. It'll have you saying I do to somebody you barely know because it needs to be satisfied."

"You don't have to tell me. Although I knew I didn't want a relationship, pain caused me to break a few hearts along the way trying to mask it."

"What made you stop?" I inquire.

"A sexual harassment claim," he admits.

"Wow."

"Yeah, it was a nightmare which caused me to miss six weeks of work. In the end, she admitted to lying but not before almost ruining everything I'd work for. Afterwards, I swore off any kind of relationship and it's been almost a year."

"May I offer you dessert?" the server asks.

He looks at me, I decline, and he gives his card to pay.

"Has divorce been harder for you being a marriage counselor?" he questions.

"Like you wouldn't imagine. I questioned how I missed the signs of my husband not being happy, although I know you can be everything and they'll still cheat. The hardest part, finding who I was without him."

"So, what advice would you give yourself?"

"The same I gave a client a few weeks back. I'm taking this as my season to shed, knowing I'll bloom again because divorce didn't take my identity, I simply need to believe in who I am again."

"That's great advice."

"It is, isn't it." I laugh grabbing my purse.

When we make it to my car, it gets awkward.

"What do we do now?" he laughs.

"Say goodnight. I don't know. It's been forever since I've been out on a date." I tell him. "However, I can say I had a great time. Thank you for a wonderful evening."

He kisses me on the forehead. "Would it be too much to ask for a text or call to let me know you made it home?"

"Of course not."

"Drive safe."

"You too."

Chapter 30

Pulling up at home, I see Angelique's car in the driveway. Walking in, the three of them are sitting in the living room.

"How was it?" they all ask.

"Why are y'all still here? Shouldn't you be at home with your men?"

"Girl, they are fine. Tell us about your date."

"It wasn't a date." I correct kicking off my shoes. "But it was great. We went to Seasons 52."

"Fancy," Sharda cuts in. "Okay, continue."

"He's been divorced for two years, no children, general surgeon and handsome. He has a younger brother, mother and grandmother. He loves to travel, read and work in the yard."

"That's it? Y'all didn't make out or nothing?" Sharda asks.

"Girl, I haven't been divorced a full 24 hours. I think I'll wait on the making out."

"Your ex didn't." She adds.

"He may not have, but I'm not him and I will not allow his actions to push me into something which could potentially cause more damage. Me and the broken pieces of my heart will be good being alone for a while."

"Well here." Angelique says. "For those nights you get lonely."

I open the box and pull out a thing shaped like a rose. "What is it?"

"A little piece of Heaven." Denise says causing Sharda and Angelique to laugh.

"A vibrator?" I whisper.

"Why are you whispering? Yes, a vibrator and it's waterproof."

"Y'all need Jesus." I tell them putting it back in the box.

"Then give it back."

I slap her hand. "I didn't say all that."

They laugh.

After letting the girls out and taking a shower, I'm getting into bed when Haven Facetimes me.

"Hey. What are you doing?"

"Getting into bed. What are you doing?"

"Going over a presentation for work tomorrow. How was your date?"

I drop my face into my hand. "It wasn't a date. Who told you?"

"I'll never reveal my sources. However, I have it on good authority you were fine and smelling good."

"Oh, I was." I smile. "Still wasn't a date."

"Did you get your gift?"

"You knew about it?" My face has probably turned five shades of red.

"Why are you embarrassed? Having a rose is better than getting your heart broke, catching a STD or HIV and you don't have to talk to it unless you want too."

"You have one?"

"No, I have three of them. There's different varieties."

"Okay, I'm not talking about vibrators with my child." I tell her. "Let's change the subject. How's your project going?"

"It's going great. In fact, if all goes well, I may be traveling to Japan for a few weeks in August. You should come with me."

"To Japan?"

"Yeah. We're working on a new Japanese animation and the bosses think going there to see the culture, in person, will help. I'm excited because it'll be a nice change of scenery and a paid vacation. Just think about it." Someone calls her name. "Ma, I gotta go. I'll call you tomorrow. Love you."

"I love you too."

I lay the phone down and get my journal.

July 14, 2020

10:10 PM

I'm officially divorced ... and I don't know how to feel. On one hand, I'm happy for it to be over. On the other, it makes everything final.

I'm a divorcee.

Wow. Never thought I'd be writing this.

Wondah Renee Parker ~~Jennings~~.

I can scratch a line through my last name on paper, but what about real life? Do I drop it or keep it? Dropping it will mean changing everything from my driver's license to the name on my certifications.

Why keep it though?

I push the journal away, grabbing my phone and opening Safari.

Searching, 'should a woman change her name after divorce'

"Many women realize they don't want to reset their entire social life. Others may feel changing your name after a divorce is a bigger part of an overall fresh start." I read out loud. "Ugh."

I throw the phone down, turn out the light and slide under the cover. Staring up at the darkness, tears begin to fall.

*****

The following Saturday, I'm sitting on the patio of my sister's house watching the kids jump into the pool. It's Denise and Daniel's seventeenth wedding anniversary and she decided to have an impromptu pool party. I look around at Denise who's helping her husband with the food, Sharda is dancing with her husband and Angelique is giggling at something her husband is whispering in her ear.

I take my phone and open Facebook. Posting one of the pictures from the other day, I add the caption …

A few months ago, I almost lost who I was. Nah, I did lose me. Heart break will do that. See, pain caused me to lash out and do things out of character. When faced with the sudden action of divorce, I didn't know who I was, and the enemy used it against me. Oh, but I'm back now and if I had to give myself a bit of advice, it'd be this. Wondah, divorce didn't take your identity, you simply need to believe in who you are again. Your identity wasn't created with marriage and it won't be destroyed by divorce.

#HappilyDivorced #Free #SurvivingMenandMe

I click post.

"Auntie, come swim with us." My great nephew Lil Chad says from the pool.

I stand, remove my swimming cover and dive in.

Making it back to the edge, I pull myself up to see a gorgeous set of eyes watching me.

He extends his hand to help me out.

"Dr. Cartwright." I smile.

"Dr. Parker." He says.

Chapter 31

Over the next two months, things have been okay. I've been sleeping a little more and finding my way back to a normal way of life, by myself. After spending a week with Haven in Japan, I realized she was right. The change of scenery was needed.

Alonzo and I have become good friends and although we've hung out a few times and gone on dates, we both decided to not pursue a dating relationship. For me, I'm not mentally or emotionally ready to give myself to another man. I've been journaling and spending time alone finding who I am. I can say, it's been harder than I expected.

Being a marriage counselor, I'm the person in the chair mediating between a husband and wife who are contemplating divorce. I'm the therapist talking a wife off the ledge when depression found its way to the side of the bed once occupied by her husband. I'm the one giving therapy to a husband sitting across from me when his wife cheated with his best friend. It's always been me in the chair and never in any stretch of my thinking and understanding, did I ever find I'd be the one on the couch.

"Wondah, did you hear me?" Dr. Holiday asks.

"I apologize, I didn't."

"I asked how you've been managing since the divorce."

"It's been a slow process Dr. Holiday. Some days, I seem to manage fine and others, my emotions hit like a gut punch. I didn't realize how much harder the holidays would make things. Labor Day, we'd normally spend it on a lake and every year, I don't schedule sessions during that time. I forgot to change it this year and without anything to do, my mind was working overtime. However, I made it through."

"What are you doing to prepare for the next holidays?"

"Making sure I have something to do." I chuckle.

"What if you don't? You have to be able to make it through without needing something to distract you. If not, you'll find yourself becoming dependent on the distractions which will then become disruptions. This is how unhealthy behaviors are formed."

"I know and I'm trying."

"How?"

"I've been journaling, boxing, taking walks and becoming more involved in church."

"Distractions." She states. "What are you doing for your mental?"

"Coming to you." I answer.

"What about when you're home alone and the darkness is speaking to you or when the memories of the past jolts you from your sleep? How do you cope with them?"

"I play music and pray."

"Have you seen your ex-husband?" she probes.

"Nope and have no plans too."

"Do you follow him on social media?"

"What does this have to do with my mental?"

"If you were counseling you, would you tell yourself a conversation with your ex is needed for closure?"

"No, because he doesn't have the power to close the wound he opened, not when he was the one who inflicted the pain. That's like him cutting me open, watching me bleed almost to death then I'm expecting him to stitch me up and nurse me back to health. He can't be the one who hurts and heals. I have to decide when and where closure happens."

"When and where does it happen?"

"When my wound is healed enough to be closed. I'm sorry Dr. Holiday, I thought coming here was needed, but I seem to be answering my own questions."

"Is that a bad thing?"

"Come to think of it, I guess it's better than talking to and answering myself."

"What's next for you? How do you see yourself in a year?"

"I don't know and honestly, I'm hesitant to think about it because when I made plans for 2020, it included a husband. Nobody could have told me differently. Yet, I find myself being on the receiving end of therapy because life threw some blows, I wasn't able to block."

"Life has a way of doing this Wondah and although we have no way of knowing when it'll happen, we can be sure it will. It doesn't matter whether it's divorce, death or change. When it comes, we have to learn to adjust. So, I'll ask again. How do you see yourself in a year?"

"Hopefully healed."

"Why not just healed?"

"Because I can be honest with myself and say it may take longer than a year for me to recover. Dr. Holiday, I'm fifty years old and was married to a man more than the time I've been single. Every milestone I hit in my adult life, I did it with him. I wasn't a promiscuous girl. I didn't have twenty relationships before him. I met him when I was twenty-one and married at twenty-four. I thought only death would separate us and for a long time, he made me believe it. I'm being realistic when I say, a year may not be long enough."

"Wondah, please don't misunderstand my line of questioning. I'm happy you're taking the time to heal without rushing it because often times, as women, we don't. Our mind tells us, after we've endured trials and tribulations, to get up. Society says, you're a woman, you're strong so girl get up, you got this. Men see women getting up within hours after birthing a baby because her body is making milk needed for their survival even though her body is not yet healed. During sickness, barely breathing we'll get up because somebody is counting on us. We can be hurt and will overlook our wound to help somebody else because women have the heart of a nurturer. This is why some boneheaded men will hurt you and walk away without a care because they think you'll be okay. And you know what some women do? We prove them right by hiding our pain."

"But isn't this what the Bible says in Proverbs 31 when it says, she makes linen and sells them because strength and honor are her clothing?"

"Yes, referring to the strength and honor of her character, not her physical body because baby, even the strongest can be weak. Wondah, my point is this. Take all the time you need to heal in order to get back to the strong woman you are. However, in the midst of your healing, there needs to be a conversation with the one who hurt you."

I shake my head.

"No, hear me out. You don't need a conversation for closure. The conversation is to hold him accountable for his action by letting him know, you may have hurt me, but you didn't destroy me. You hurt me because I'm human, but you couldn't destroy me because I'm God's. Holding him or anyone else accountable for their actions may make them rethink doing the same thing to somebody else."

"I'll think about it."

"Good."

"Thank you, Dr. Holiday. I'll see you next week."

Chapter 32

Three months later

"Mommy," Haven screams when I walk out of the airport. "I'm so happy you're here."

"Hey baby. I'm happy to be here although I'm not sure how to feel about celebrating Christmas in seventy-degree weather. Do y'all even sell stuff for the traditional dinner, like turkeys?"

She helps to put my suitcase in the trunk.

"I think so." She chuckles as we get in the car. "I talked to Auntie Denise. She said they'll be here later tonight."

"I know, she sent a text. I missed you." I say touching her hand.

"I missed you too." She gets quiet.

"What?"

"I know we usually spend Labor Day at a lake and with everything, I was worried about you being alone."

"You don't have to worry. It was good to spend some time alone and start new traditions."

"What did you do?"

"Nothing." I laugh. "No, I stayed around the house and binged watched the series Zoo on Netflix."

"Zoo?"

"Yeah, it's about animals taking over the world because they no longer fear humans. It's pretty good."

"You watch some strange stuff." She scrunches her nose. "You need a hobby."

"I have a hobby, it's called a job."

"I'm talking about something fun and I don't mean another remodeling job at the house. Speaking of, have you seen dad?" she asks me.

"Uh no. I haven't seen him since he moved out and I want to keep it that way."

"He's not with Anette anymore. The baby wasn't his."

"Good for the baby."

I see her look at me out the corner of my eye. "Tell me about this house you found." I reply, changing the subject.

She smiles. "You're going to love it."

Twenty minutes later, we pull up to an estate. "Oh my God Haven, this is gorgeous."

"See, I told you. It belongs to one of my bosses and he's allowing us to use it this week."

"Dang girl, you get perks like this?"

"I call it favor. It's been in his family since he was little, and they only use it for parties and holidays. He heard me say I was looking for a vacation house and offered it to me. It would've been crazy to turn it down. Besides, it gives all of us a chance to spend Christmas together outside of Memphis."

"Don't act like you don't love being home."

"I do, but ma, we can swim, eat turkey and dressing and exchange gifts at the same time. How cool is that?"

"You do have a point."

I get my suitcase and walk up the stairs. Reaching for the door, it opens.

"Aw hell no." I say when Harvey is standing there with a beer in his hand.

"You should have told me he'd be here." I state throwing my suitcase on the bed. "I asked if you'd seen him."

"Would it have mattered?" she asks. "You were still coming."

"Yes, it would have mattered because I could have prepared myself to see his ugly ass."

"Ma come on. It's been over six months. Can you put your disagreement aside for the week?"

"Oh, is that what we're calling what he did? It was a disagreement. Humph. I thought it was an unexpected divorce, cheating, a new baby and flat out disrespect. However, my bad. Maybe you know something I don't."

"I didn't mean it, I'm sorry. I only want us to enjoy Christmas since we didn't spend Thanksgiving together."

"Then you shouldn't have allowed me to be blindsided by him being here. Look Haven, I have no problem being in the same room with your father. However, these eight months," I correct, "doesn't miraculously dissolve the kind of pain he unleashed onto me and being caught off guard brought back everything I thought I'd dealt with. How would you have felt if I allowed you to open a door with a clown standing behind it, something you're afraid of, and didn't warn you?"

"You aren't afraid of daddy."

"You're missing the point Haven. Without warning you, the clown could have caused you an anxiety attack. However, knowing would give you time to mentally prepare." I sigh. "Just forget it."

"I'm sorry. I didn't think it would be this big of a deal. Do you want me to ask him to leave?"

"No. Close the door on the way out."

"Ma—

"Haven, it's fine."

She closes the door and I walk over to the window overlooking the backyard. Sitting on the bench, I close my eyes.

"Lord, don't allow me to go back to the darkness of anger and pain."

I think back to the time I've spent at Release. I started to go there after the divorce was final and I finished removing everything of Harvey from my life, including his name on the deed of the house. He moved out on July 15th and I had a construction company there on July 20th remodeling the man cave, office and the guest room.

"Wondah, we're in the locker room and you have to decide what you're changing out of today." AJ points to the sign on the wall. NO MATTER WHAT, I'M _____. "What's yours today?"

"No matter what, I'm fighting."

"What are you fighting?"

"Not what, who. I'm fighting the flesh of me in order for my will to survive, my heart to heal, my mind to be restored, my eyes to see beyond the present, my faith to sustain and for who I am. I've spent the last four months fighting with anger and now I need to fight through it in order for Wondah to survive."

She touches my hand. "Wondah, like last time we start in the locker room not for you to change clothes, but to transform your view on what you've brought to release. Again, this is your safe space to undress mentally without worrying about judgment. All I ask is for you to give your release all you have. Can you do that?"

"I have too."

"Good. Then let's get to work."

She walks me to the boxing floor. Standing in front of the punching bag, she wraps my hands. As she wraps, she speaks.

"I speak power into your hands. I speak you will find your strength again. I speak joy will push out all sorrow, light will overshadow every point of darkness and hope will abound. With every punch of this bag, release what was because your next is waiting. With every punch to this bag, release the pain and heal. With every punch, release the stronghold of anger. With every punch, command your release."

She turns me around to the bag.

"You have the power and the punch. Release it."

I stretch my neck, not bothering about the tears.

"Take your stance and release it." She tells me.

I get into position and raise my hands. Throwing a punch, she grabs the bag.

"Wondah, you can't hurt this bag, but you can hurt yourself by holding in what doesn't belong. Release it." She screams.

I punch again.

"Release it. It doesn't deserve you."

I punch harder.

"Release it. It has no power."

"Ah," I yell punching the bag again.

"Release it. It can no longer have its way in your life."

I punch.

"Release it. It tried but didn't win."

I begin punching the bag over and over, screaming and crying until I fall down to my knees.

Tears, I didn't even realize were falling, hits my hand pulling me from my thoughts.

"Get it together Wondah. You are the only one who can give your power away. You're stronger than you believe, and you don't have to forget, but you do have to forgive."

Chapter 33

"Uh, did you know he was going to be here?" Denise whispers when Harvey walks out onto the patio after dinner.

"No."

"So, Harvey, where's your baby?" Sharda blurts out. "The newborn, not your girlfriend."

He looks at her with daggers and she stares back.

"The baby wasn't mine."

"Well, gat damn." She laughs.

"Okay, you've had enough of this." Her husband Chad says taking her glass.

"I'm not drunk. I only asked because Harvey wasn't shy about posting his new love all over social media with pictures and memes. Until, boom," Sharda whips out her phone. "She pops out with a new baby and husband."

Denise snatches the phone. "So, this chick lied and strung you along an entire pregnancy only for you not to be the pappy?"

"How did you find out? Did she leave papers?" I ask sipping my drink.

"Karma ate that ass up, didn't it?" Sharda laughs. "Serves you right. You chose a child over thirty years of marriage to a woman. Yeah, you deserve all of this."

"What do you know about what I deserve?" he barks. "I wasn't married to you."

"Negro, you were married to the family and when you hurt my aunt, you hurt me too. She didn't deserve what you did and for you to sit here like all is forgiven without saying anything is disgusting. I'm glad the baby wasn't yours. You didn't need another life to ruin."

"Sharda, that's enough." I tell her. "I don't need an apology or conversation from dude because it will not change how I've lived and will live my life going forward. His lack of an apology isn't keeping me stagnant or bound. I'm good." I admit never taking my eyes off him.

"I did apologize." He says. "However, whatever conversation Wondah and I need to have is between us."

"Uh, no boo. There's no conversation needed. See, although my therapist advised me to tell you how hurt you left me, you already know this. So, just to reiterate. There is no needed conversation sir. You had ample time to talk to me before the divorce and after. You chose not to. In fact, you walked around like I was the one who'd done you wrong, never uttering a single word. Keep it like that."

"I knew you were angry."

"You're damn right I was angry, by your actions. All of this is because of you. You made love to me the night before handing me copies of papers dissolving our marriage and told me to be amicable about it. Now, your excuse is, I knew you'd be angry. Dude, you're a whole joke."

"I think we need to let them talk." Daniel, Denise's husband says standing up.

"No, please stay. You all were the ones who helped me when he walked away. Y'all saw me at my lowest when my husband strolled his monkey ass out of the life, we spent years creating like his retirement came early and it was his last day on the job. Don't spare him the embarrassment of this conversation. Stay here and look at the face of a sad, pathetic piece of shit."

"You can call me all the names you like, I'm not leaving. I have a right to spend the holidays with my daughter the same as you."

"Nobody asked you to leave, SpongeBob." Sharda states.

"She's right." I add. "Nobody said you had to leave. However, did you really think things would go smoothly with you here? Don't answer because it's obvious you did. What happened to you?"

"What are you talking about?" he asks after sipping his drink.

"What happened to turn you into this?" I ask moving my hand up and down. "You've become a stranger."

"People can change without needing anyone's approval." He shrugs. "I changed and realized I wanted more."

"Wow." Denise says.

"Well, I need to thank you." I tell him.

"For what?" he inquires.

"For sparing me from the new you. Your leaving was a blessing I didn't even know I needed because who you are now, I could never love."

"Okay, can we please stop this." Haven yells. "This isn't my idea of a nice family Christmas. I get things ended badly and I'm still mad at daddy for how he handled things, but don't we have enough to be grateful for? Mom, you cut your foot and could have bled to death. Daddy, you were in an accident and it could have killed you. Sharda and Auntie Denise, we have things to be thankful for. Things like me moving to Japan for a year."

"Wait, what?" I scream. "Oh my God Haven."

"It's why I wanted us all here." She tears up. "Mom, I'm sorry for not telling you daddy would be here. Will you forgive me?"

"Of course, I forgive you." I stand to give her a hug. "Japan though, for a year. When are you leaving?"

"January twelfth."

"Haven, I apologize for my part in this." Harvey looks at me. "Going forward, I will do whatever I can to make this as peaceful as possible."

He gives her a hug and when her back is to me, I throw him a finger sign.

Later into the night after way too many of Sharda's concoction of a pink vodka lemonade, I slip into Harvey's room.

"Wondah—

"Hush." I order. "All I need is sex."

"I don't think this is right."

"Your penis doesn't care what you think and neither do I." I drop my robe and climb on top of him.

Sometime later, I open my eyes to see dude asleep next to me. I slip out of bed, put my robe back on and go into the bathroom. When I'm done, I look through the nightstand for a pen and paper. Finding what I need, I leave a note before going back to my room.

The next morning, he burst into my bathroom.

"What is this?" he throws the paper at me.

"You can't read? It's a divorce note. Doesn't feel good to have your stuff taken and then be left, huh?"

"You did this as payback?"

"Payback would mean I care enough about your feelings and I don't."

"Yet, you snuck into my room last night to ride my—

"I did, and it was really good." I interrupt smiling. "However, it was solely for my satisfaction seeing it's been over seven months and you're the only man I've been with in thirty years."

"You should have called your doctor boyfriend."

"Yeah, I could have but you were here and a safe option for a warm penis and a few orgasms. Thank you. You can go now."

He walks closer to me. "This is the one time I wish I had a STD."

"Good thing I know how much pride you take in your health."

"You were the one talking all that shit last night about me being a stranger and blessings. Yet, I wasn't strange enough for you to sleep with."

"Dude, I said you'd changed, not him." I point to his private area. "Now, if you're mad, I pulled a you on you, just say it so we can end this already because I need a shower and coffee."

He throws a finger sign and I blow a kiss before he stomps out.

"Heifer," Denise pulls me into her when I walk into the kitchen. "Did I hear you and Harvey last night?"

"Yeah, it was only sex though. I left him a divorce sticky note on the nightstand."

Sharda spits her coffee out.

"And he's big mad."

We all burst into laughing when Haven comes in from the pool. I go over to get coffee.

"What are y'all up too?" She asks.

"Nothing. What's for breakfast, I'm starving?"

Chapter 34

Christmas Eve; CJ, Shad and Sofie, Sharda's children are helping Haven decorate a small tree we were able to find half off. Sharda is passing out drinks, while Denise and Daniel are dancing to Whitney Houston's, "I Wanna Dance with Somebody". Harvey hasn't come downstairs since we've been home from lunch and shopping, and no one is complaining.

My phone rings with a Facetime from Angelique. I get my cigar and lighter and head outside.

"Sister, how are you enjoying Australia?" I ask when it connects.

"Believe it or not, I love it. It's not at all what I expected. Look." She says panning the phone. "Isn't this beautiful?"

"Oh my God, Angel, it is."

"I'm only mad I hadn't gotten Ethan to bring us here sooner. Tomorrow, we're going to a place called Bondi Beach. It's where most celebrate Christmas here. Who would have thought you could enjoy Christmas on a beach?" She chuckles. "Anyway, how's your holiday in California?"

"I slept with Harvey." I blurt closing the door to the patio and walking down the stairs to sit near the pool.

"Shit," Angelique says fumbling to catch her phone. "Girl hold on because my phone was so shocked, it jumped out my hands."

"Hell, even I was shocked, but I needed the release, he was here and a safe option."

"And what now? Is this going to be an occasional thing, hooking up with him because he's safe? Wondah, we both know what this can turn into."

"It was only this one time. I don't like him and have no plans to sleep with him again."

"You don't have to like him, nor make plans yet it doesn't stop your body from craving that man's touch now it's been reawakened in you. Wondah, you're still healing from the heartbreak he caused and blurring the lines now can be disastrous."

"I know, please don't lecture me."

"Obviously, you needed me too or you wouldn't have told me."

"I told you because I didn't want big mouth Sharda to."

"You can try and convince yourself, all you want. However, as your friend and a licensed therapist, you told me because you need me to talk your flesh out of going back. Wondah, he's the man you've loved majority of your life and him being there reminds you of the familiar, the comfort and the what was. In those moments, your heart resonates the hurt, but your flesh wants gratification, so it'll press it down. All I'm saying is, don't fall into the bed of comfort satisfying the temptation, only to wake up with the weight of a burden you'll spend the next year trying to break."

I look away.

"Sister look at me. If you want to sleep with your ex-husband, you're grown and can. However, I wouldn't be a great best friend if I didn't point out the danger in doing so. Your wound is still fresh and reopening it could be detrimental to your health."

I close my eyes as tears begin to fall. "I miss the familiar." I cry. "As much as he hurt me, my heart still searches for him. When he walks in the room, my eyes instinctively gravitate towards him. I can tell when he's close because my body signals that he is. I had to stop myself from preparing his plate at breakfast or asking if he needs anything. This man hurt me—

"And you still love him." She finishes.

"This isn't fair."

"Wondah, no one is blaming you for still loving Harvey. Even if you told me you didn't, I wouldn't believe it because it's hard to erase thirty years."

"Maybe someone should come up with a pill to erase your memories like the Plan B." I laugh wiping my face. "I'm sorry for dropping this on you while you're enjoying time with your family."

"That's what sisters do, right? Girl, I'm always here for you."

"Thank you, I love you and Merry Christmas. Tell Ethan and the girls too. We'll talk more after the holidays."

"I will. Merry Christmas and I love you too."

I end the call and lay the phone down.

"God, I've made a mess of things. Help me not to fall into temptation. My spirit is willing, but Jesus my flesh is weak. Help me Father."

After everyone is gone to bed, I'm in the kitchen preparing cornbread for tomorrow's turkey and dressing, potatoes for the potato salad and sweet potato pies. My phone is propped up on the sink, playing "If Only You Knew" by Patti Labelle.

Closing the oven, I close my eyes as Patti's voice serenades the room.

I dream of moments we share, but you're not there. I'm living in a fantasy cause you don't even suspect, could probably care less about the changes I've been going through.

"You're telling my story Patti."

I turn, shocked to see Harvey standing there.

"I didn't mean to scare you. I came to get something to drink and seeing you like this reminds me—

"Don't." I stop him. "I don't need you to bring anything to my remembrance because unlike you, it's been hard for me to forget."

"What makes you think this has been easy for me?"

"I'm not doing this with you. Get your drink and go. Please."

He walks closer to me. "Wondah, stay in my room tonight." He whispers in my ear.

"And then what? We fly home to Memphis and you go back to treating me like I don't exist until you're horny again?"

"Is that not what you did?"

"You're right and I apologize for sleeping with you the other night. I gave you the idea it could happen again, and it won't."

"Come on. I'm not asking for a relationship, it's just sex between two people who know each other."

"No, it's also my sanity. Dude, you hurt me and although it's been easy for you to walk away and act as if the last thirty years of our life didn't exist, I can't. These last eight months have been some of the hardest I've had to survive and sleeping with you only makes things worse for me mentally. So, we can be cordial for the next three days, but that's it."

I step back, and he gets a bottle of water and leaves. When he does, I look up towards the ceiling and exhale.

Chapter 35

"Merry Christmas Ma." Haven says coming into the kitchen to give me a hug. "It smells good in here."

"Merry Christmas baby. Thank you. Breakfast is almost done."

"Did you sleep?" she questions raising the top off the pies.

I shrug.

"Ma, are you okay?"

"Of course."

"No, I mean for real? I know it's been hard having daddy here especially knowing Christmas is your favorite holiday. You'd have us in matching pajamas and a hundred pictures taken by now."

"Yeah, but things and people change. Nevertheless, Christmas is still my favorite holiday and although it looks different than what I'm used too, I'm happy."

I remove the pan of biscuits from the oven.

"Let everybody know breakfast is ready."

Once we're done eating, the kitchen has been cleaned and the turkey put in the oven; we sit around the floor of the living room to open presents.

"Me first," Denise says handing me and Sharda identical boxes.

We tear the paper off and open them to reveal a onesie. *You're going to make a great aunt.*

"Denise? Oh my God, you're pregnant?"

She stands up, pulling her shirt back.

"Five months." She beams.

I throw the box down and rush to her with Sharda jumping up and down. Denise and Daniel have been trying to have a baby for over seven years. When she turned forty-one last year, she said they were giving up and trying adoption.

"I thought y'all were no longer trying." I say wiping the tears.

"We weren't." She says looking at Daniel. "This is all God. Our baby girl is healthy and will be here in May."

"I'm happy for you two. Oh my God." Sharda squeals.

It takes a minute before everyone settles down. Haven hands me another box.

"Wait," I say to her.

"Oh no, I'm definitely not pregnant." She laughs.

I open the box to find a reloadable journal with Wondah Renee Jennings stenciled on the front. Flipping back the cover, there's a quote on the inside.

"Celebrate endings, for they precede new beginnings." – Jonathan Lockwood Huie.

"I love it." I tell her. "Thank you."

"This is for you." I say to Harvey. "I ordered it way before, well I couldn't send it back and there's nothing I can do with it, so here."

He rips open the package to find a gold toned stethoscope engraved with his name and Colossians three verse fourteen.

"Wow. Thank you."

"Who's next?" I ask.

Before dinner, Harvey comes up to me.

"Above all, clothe yourselves with love, which binds us all together in perfect harmony." He says.

"What?"

"Colossians three, fourteen."

I nod and begin to walk off.

"Wondah, I'm sorry."

I sigh and turn back.

"I'm sorry for hurting you and I truly mean it. Will you forgive me?"

"When you looked up the scripture, did you read verse thirteen?"

"No."

"It says to make allowances for each other's faults and forgive anyone who offends you. Harvey," he smiles. "I ain't there yet though."

✹✹✹✹✹

Sunday afternoon, on the plane, I put my headphones in to listen to service from this morning. When Pastor Brielle gives her title, I roll my eyes.

"Really God?"

"Excuse me." The gentleman says sitting next to me. I point to my headphones.

"A few months back, I preached from Matthew six, where Jesus is teaching about fasting and prayer. I told you then you have to forgive your debtor. Debtor as in the person who owes you but has yet to make amends. And yes, here I am again today talking about forgiveness because it's the thing most of us are caught up in and don't even know it. We think we're in a storm when we're really stagnant because we've yet to forgive others.

Every day we walk around harboring feelings of bitterness towards people who've done us wrong. Every time you see them, your mind instantly reverts to thinking negative or hostile thoughts towards them. You can't even make a status on Facebook without it dripping with drama because all your mind know is hatefulness. Why? You've yet to forgive folk or here's a hard truth, you've yet to forgive you.

You think you don't need to forgive folk, just move on and leave them. You think you don't need the forgiveness of people when you can act like they don't exist. You feel as though people have to earn your forgiveness, when here's the truth of the matter. Lean in people of God and receive this. Forgiveness isn't for them, it's for you. Baby, I don't know about you, but I don't have space to not forgive. I don't have time to consistently think about what you did to me. I don't have time to continually lay awake at night, mad at you while you're off living the best of your life.

Here's what I'm going to gift you with this Christmas. I'm giving you the gift of forgiveness. We don't have to speak, I'm not accepting your friend request on Facebook or unblocking you, but I forgive you. Not for you, for me. See, when I don't forgive you, it's messing up my relationship with God because forgiveness is restoring relationship on Earth, the eternal stuff God handles.

Forgiveness is for restoring fellowship right here on earth, because God got Heaven covered. Forgiveness, if done properly can make family functions less tense. Forgiveness, if handled the right way, can restore in a matter of minutes what years of unforgiveness have stolen from you. And I know Christmas was two days ago and while some of you spent more than you should on tangible gifts, the real gift you need to give before 2020 ends is forgiveness.

Truth is, there are some families, instead of exchanging gifts, you need to exchange apologies. There're some relationships, even if you never go back to being best friends, that need to be restored by forgiving. Forgiveness allows fellowship. I don't mean bringing up old issues but sitting down and having a real adult conversation beginning with, forgive me. Or here's an even harder one, I forgive you. Yeah, I know some of you are ready to check out of this message, that's okay, the message will still be the same when you catch the replay.

Brothers and sisters, you cannot keep walking around here spiritually dead because unforgiveness is sucking the life out of you. The stench you smell, it's coming from your spirit that's been tainted by the pollution of unforgiveness. It's been in there so long, if someone would do an x-ray, it'd probably look like a third lung and you don't even know how to live without it. You've been so mad, for so long you don't know how to function without it. You've been divorced 22 years and you still find something negative to say about your ex because of what they did or didn't do.

You think you can pick and choose, how and when to give forgiveness. Forgiveness isn't an option. Boo, Jesus says if you forgive folk for their trespasses, He'll forgive you. We seem to think forgiveness is a choice, naw baby, forgiveness isn't an option, it's obedience."

I press the home button to close Facebook, dropping the phone in my lap.

Once the plane has landed, I remove my phone from airplane mode, unblock Harvey and send a text.

Me: I forgive you. Wondah.

Placing him back on the block list, I exhale, determined to move on.

Chapter 36

Three weeks later, the doorbell rings as I'm getting my things to leave for church. Opening it, there's a vase of my favorite flowers. Calla Lilies. Bringing them inside, I remove the card.

You came to me like the dawn through the night. Just shinin' like the sun out of my dreams and into my life. You are the one. Said I loved you, but I lied.

I flip it over.

Happy Anniversary Babe. Love you forever and a lifetime. Harvey.

I pull up in the church parking lot, barely putting the car in park. Snatching the vase and power walking to the door in my dress and tennis shoes, I don't mind anyone who's staring.

"Wondah. Wondah." I hear Denise behind me. "What's wrong?"

Walking down the hall towards the Sunday school classes, I begin to yell Harvey's name.

"Wondah, stop." She pulls me into an empty classroom. "What is wrong with you?"

"Denise, let me go."

The door opens and Pastor Brielle, Harvey and Deacon Johnson file in. When Harvey steps away from them, I throw the vase towards his head.

"I forgave you and this is what you do? I forgave you and you send me this." I throw the card. "After everything you've put me through, you'd do this. Do you hate me that much? Am I a joke to you?"

Denise's hand covers her mouth as she reads the card.

"What are you talking about?" Harvey asks.

"Why? Huh? Why send my favorite flowers and a sick note like this on today of all days? Twenty-eight years and this is all I'm worth to you? I gave you everything." I scream.

"Flowers, oh my God. I didn't cancel the anniversary flowers. Wondah, it was an honest mistake."

"This is no mistake, bastard. You took the time to dictate a message so cruel and evil even for you."

He takes the card from Pastor Brielle.

"No, no." He shakes his head. "This isn't what it looks like. I'm sorry."

I walk over to him and punch him square in the face. When he doubles over, I begin to kick him everywhere my foot lands until Deacon Johnson pulls me away. I snatch from him and open the door, letting it hit the wall.

"I hope the next time you face death, God doesn't spare your life."

Sometime later, I'm sitting in my car at Tom Lee Park with the largest bottle of Hennessy the liquor store sold. When I left the house earlier, all I grabbed was my wallet and key fob.

"Said I loved you, but I lied." I keep repeating as tears stream from my eyes. "God." I hit the steering wheel. I press the power button, turning off the ignition. I get out with the bottle and begin to walk down the hill towards the river.

"Ma'am are you okay?" a young man running by asks. I keep walking. Getting to the edge, I sit on the ground. Twisting the top, I chug it. Looking out on the water, I continue to drink from the bottle.

"Are you okay?" someone else asks.

"Hell no and stop asking." I yell turning around and no one is there. When I move, the bottle falls and rolls too far for me to reach. "Damn it." Putting my head into my hands, I hear someone say, "go home." I raise up and look around.

"Go home."

I start to laugh.

"You don't get to tell me what to do." I refute.

Being stubborn, I stay seated in the grass. It starts to rain, and I shake my head.

"Really?" I continue to sit there until I'm shaking from the cold. Finally, prying myself up, I make it to my truck. Getting inside, I start it and lay my head back.

Pulling up at home, Angelique runs to the truck. Opening the door, she doesn't say anything. Instead, she turns off the ignition, grabs my hand and pulls me out. Leading me to my bedroom, she pushes me into the bathroom. Turning on the water, she comes over to unbutton my dress before bending down to untie my tennis shoes.

"Raise your foot. Now, this one."

My dress drops, and I feel her removing my bra and underwear.

She opens the door of the shower. "Get in."

She removes her shoes and steps in behind me. When she begins to wash my body, I break and slide down into the floor. She catches me, wrapping her arms around me.

"How can he hate me so much?"

"Harvey doesn't hate you."

"God. How can God hate me? I've done things, but not enough to deserve this. Am I this bad of a person that He'd allow this much pain?"

"You're going through a battle, but God hasn't left you nor does He hate you."

Her arms tighten, and I let out a sob.

I blink a few times, realizing I'm home although I'm not sure how I got here. I look under the cover and I'm in pajamas. Early morning light is shining through the window and with the headache piercing, I close my eyes trying to remember …

Flowers

Church

Sitting in the park

Drinking

The note … Said I loved you, but I lied.

Exhaling, I roll over and dang near jump out the bed when I see Angelique smiling at me.

"What are you doing here?"

"Where else would I be?" she asks.

"Right, like who do you take us for?" Sharda pops up from the foot of the bed.

"You really should know us by now." Denise yawns from the other side of Angelique.

I put my hand over my eyes. "What time is it?"

"Six nineteen in the morning. Too early to be up." Sharda yawns.

"Go home to your families," I tell them.

"No need, they're all here."

My hand drops and when I open my mouth, a heavy sigh comes out followed by tears. "I can't expect y'all to put your life on hold for me. I appreciate each of you being here, but it's Monday and I know you have to work. Sharda—

"Gul, hush. We got this covered." She counters.

"Wondah, let's say I'm in a boat that hit a rock causing a hole and water is pouring in. You're walking by, see me struggling to get back to shore because if I don't, I might not survive. Would you keep on by leaving me to fend for myself?"

"Of course not."

"Then what makes you think we'll leave you struggling to get back to shore? Yes, we all have lives, we also have hearts and you need us."

"I don't like being needy, though."

"Hell, who does?" Angelique probes.

"Mommy," Sofie calls from outside the door.

"Duty calls." Sharda raises up. "I'll start breakfast."

"I'll help." Angelique says.

When they leave, Denise slides closer to me.

"How are you feeling?" I ask rubbing her stomach.

"We're good. How are you feeling?"

"Other than a headache and heartache, I'm great." I smile.

"I can give you something for the headache, the heartache is between you and God. You should know, Harvey was here last night."

I look at her before turning back to stare at the ceiling.

"He came to explain the flowers and I think you need to hear him out."

"The note told me all I needed to know."

"The note wasn't complete."

My forehead crease with confusion.

"I'll let him explain whenever you're ready to talk to him."

A tap on the door. "Good morning." Daniel says sticking his head in. "Babe, you have an emergency at the office."

"Go," I tell her. "I'll be fine."

Left alone, I roll onto my side and gaze out the window. "Lord, I can't do this on my own."

Chapter 37

Wednesday night, I'm at home on the couch with the lights out, candles lit and music playing. As much as I enjoy the company of family, my mind is overwhelmed, and I don't feel like talking or sharing anymore of how I'm feeling. While they are doing their best to comfort, console and encourage, their understanding is limited because they've never been through this.

Hell, I shouldn't be going through this. I shouldn't be divorced. Yet, here I am. Fifty years old and divorced. Fifty years old and starting over. Instead of making plans for early retirement, traveling and whatever else a husband and wife do after being together thirty years, I'm surrounded by darkness as I come to terms with divorce.

A divorce I didn't ask for, didn't plan for nor did I see it coming.

My phone dings with a text.

My Sister Denise: Hey, just checking to see how you are. Have you eaten?

"How am I?" I chuckle. "Yeah, Wondah how are you? Have you eaten? You good? No. I'm not good." I scream. "I'm mad. I'm heartbroken. I'm confused. I'm lost. I'm hurt. I'm devastated. I'm broken. I'm alone."

I punch the couch.

"Have you eaten?" I mock. "No, I haven't eaten. What do you eat to cure grief? What kind of vegetables are there to mend brokenness? Is there a juice I can drink to fill this hole in my heart? God!"

I stop the music playing then reply to Denise.

Me: I'm good and yes, I've eaten. Thanks for checking on me.

"God, forgive me for lying."

I stretch out on the couch staring into the quiet. Minutes pass and I begin to get antsy. Mind is in overdrive, thinking.

How do you overcome this? How soon should you overcome this? I hate him. How could he walk away from me, us? Was our entire life a lie?

"Ugh." I yell getting up, blowing out the candles and turning on the light. Snatching my laptop from the kitchen counter, I find myself perched back into the corner of the couch. Bringing up Facebook, I search my friend list for an old classmate, Georgia, who's a real estate agent. Locating her, I send a message asking her to give me a call in the morning.

"I need a change."

Opening Google, I type in Zillow and begin the search for a two to three-bedroom, two bath home. Spending over an hour, I finally come across a few I like, one especially in Olive Branch, MS. It's a little dated, however nothing a renovation budget can't fix. I'll ask Georgia about it tomorrow.

Satisfied, I close my laptop and disarm the alarm. In the garage, I grab some empty totes and newspaper I've been meaning to throw away. Back in the house, I begin removing pictures from the mantle.

Doorbell ringing.

Opening my eyes, I realize I fell asleep on the couch.

Doorbell rings again.

"Coming."

Stumbling over stuff and pulling open the door, Denise is standing there with a Starbucks cup.

"You look like you just completed the graveside shift at Regional One. Have you gotten any—uh, Wondah, what the hell happened in here."

"I'm moving."

"Moving where?"

"Somewhere other than here. I need change."

"Okay, do you even have somewhere in mind?"

"Nope."

"Then why are you packing?"

"Because I can." I yell. "Shit. Stop treating me like I'm a patient in Lakeside Behavioral Health. I know what I'm doing."

"I'm only trying to help."

I exhale. "Just back off a little. Please." I relent.

"Fine."

She sits the cup on the table, turning to leave.

"Denise, wait."

"No. I will not have you yelling at me for being here for you. You're right Wondah. I don't know how you feel, and I'd never pretend like I do. However, don't push away those of us who are in your corner."

"I'm sorry." I plop on the couch. "Y'all just don't understand what it's like to have your life shredded. My head feels as though I'm in a fog that will not clear no matter what I do and being in this house is killing me."

"What can I do?"

"Go home."

She looks at me.

"Go home Denise. You have a little girl who is depending on you and taking on my stress isn't good for either of you. I'll be fine because I've taken the next couple of weeks off and I plan on speaking to a real estate agent today. The sooner I can get the house on the market, the better."

She comes over, kissing me on the forehead. I kiss her stomach in return, pressing my cheek against it.

"She needs you to survive this." She tells me.

"I know, and I will. It's going to take some time, however I will. I love you." I tell her.

"I love you too."

An hour after she leaves, I get a call from Georgia. She's stopping by to begin the process. I straighten up the mess I created in the living room, shower and dress. When finished, I scramble two eggs and prepare a cup of coffee. Sitting at the counter, my phone rings.

I answer and press the speaker button. "Hey stranger."

"Hey yourself." Alonzo says. "How have you been?"

"Good, what about you?"

"No complaints. I was calling because I have tickets to a St. Jude fundraising event and I'd love for you to accompany me."

"When?"

"Saturday, February thirteenth. It's called Love in Action, a black-tie event."

I pause.

"I understand if it's too soon."

"No, I was making sure I didn't have plans." I lie. "I'll go with you."

"Great. I'll call or text you with additional details later. Wondah, thank you."

"Thank you for asking. I'll see you soon."

Hanging up the call, the doorbell rings.

*****

"Georgia, I can't thank you enough for coming by."

"No problem. This house is gorgeous and with the current state of the buyer's market, I'm sure it will not take long for us to sell it. I'll send my photographer by in a few days to get pictures and then we'll go from there. I also have the list of homes you want to see. I'll reach out to the agents to set up some showings. Is tomorrow too soon?"

"No ma'am, the sooner the better."

"We'll talk soon."

Once she leaves, I stand in the middle of the living room.

"Remember not the former things, nor consider the things of old. Behold, I am doing a new thing, now it springs forth, do you not perceive it? I will make a way in the wilderness and rivers in the desert. Isaiah forty-three and nineteen." I state.

Chapter 38

"Hey," I answer a Facetime call from Haven.

"Hey, where are you?"

"Getting ready to walk through a house with my real estate agent. What do you think?" I turn the camera around.

"It reminds me of a cabin. I like it."

"Me too."

"So, you're really selling the house?" she asks.

"Yep. It's been on the market for two weeks and there's already been six offers made."

"Wow. That fast."

"What's up, why are you sounding like this? Did something happen?"

"Yeah. You and daddy got divorced."

"Haven."

She starts to cry. "I don't know why it hit me all of a sudden. It's like, y'all are real deal divorced. No more French toast Saturdays, Labor Days at the lake, family vacations in Hawaii and those crazy family pictures you made us take every year. I'm so mad at daddy."

I lean against the car and allow her to get everything out.

"Where am I supposed to go when I come home? How am I supposed to drop off a grandchild to his grandparents and go missing for the entire weekend when y'all aren't even together anymore?"

"Wait, are you pregnant?"

"God, no. I'm saying. Things weren't supposed to be like this. It's always been you and daddy."

"I know sweet girl and I wish I had the answers for you."

"Mom, I'm sorry for not being there for you. Oh my God, if this hurts you half as much as it does me, I understand why you acted like you did. This hurt." She sobs.

"Haven calm down and breathe. Baby, look at me."

She takes some breaths, wiping her face with the end of her shirt. "How are you so strong?"

"Girl," I chuckle. "If only you knew. Yet, I remember my daughter singing a song, even though she can't sing worth nothing. She told me we often forfeit our peace and bear needless pain, all because we do not carry everything to God in prayer. You remember?"

She nods.

"It's because of God, family and friends I'm making it. Haven, I wish I could tell you there'd be no more days and nights of crying. I wish I could tell you things have been easy. They haven't. In fact, these last nine months have been the hardest of my life and I can choose to continue letting them be hard or I can choose peace. Sweetie, I'm choosing peace and the only way I get it is by changing the things I can and allowing God to move what I can't."

"I love you." She says.

"I love you too and I'll call you later tonight."

Pressing the phone against my chest, I close my eyes and pray for her mind.

"Wondah, are you ready?" Georgia asks.

"Yes ma'am."

Later the same night, sitting in bed with my journal.

February 5, 2021

I found a new house today and I put in an offer. Man, I never thought I'd be moving again. When this house was built twenty-five years ago, Harvey and I said it was our "forever" home. I believed him. Yet, here's what I've come to realize. People have the right to change their minds. Does it make it easier when you're the one left dazed and confused by the sudden change? No. Nonetheless, he had a right to change his mind, his marital status and his address.

Now, I have to change how I accept it because I've been the raging, angry black woman. I've drank until I passed out. I've stayed up for hours. I've gone days without a substantial meal. I've destroyed things. Hell, I almost destroyed me. You know what it did to him? Absolutely nothing. He still walked away while I sat beside the river in forty-degree weather with a fifth of Hennessy looking crazy.

Divorce hurts.

Sudden divorce hurts.

Nevertheless, I had to face reality. I'M A DIVORCEE and there's nothing I can do about it. Wait, yes there is. I can choose how I see me. I'm not Wondah Renee Jennings, divorcee. I'm Wondah Renee Jennings, single woman.

Name: Wondah Renee Jennings.

Marital status: Single.

Sunday morning, Pastor Brielle is preaching from Second Samuel nine, verses three through seven.

"What if the fall you've taken wasn't meant to punish you but position you to be chosen? What if the fall which crippled you, is also the thing that changes you? What if the thing that hurts you, turns out to be the very thing hiding you until God honors you? What if the mistake is the thing God is going to use to bless you? What if the desolate dwelling you find yourself, due to bad decisions, is the very place you'll hear God calling your name to be used? Sometimes, it's in the bleak place where there's no harvest that causes us to hold to God's unchanging hand. Sometimes, it takes us falling into a sunken place we will try God again. Sometimes, we may have to experience Lo-debar before we believe God can provide.

What if you have to experience Lo-debar, the low place until you get to your Jerusalem, the city of peace? I'm only asking because sometimes we can despise a person, place or thing that God can use to elevate us. Mephibosheth thought he'd die in a dry place, leaving no legacy for his family then, here comes a blessing he didn't know about to shift the dynamics of his living. Mephibosheth was in a dry place, but he was on the mind of the king who wanted to show him the kindness of God. Some of us, God is trying to restore what's been ours since birth. You think God has forgotten you, but what if like Mephibosheth, in Second Samuel nine, the king is about to bless you because the low place is what kept you alive?"

After service, I go up to Pastor Brielle.

"Wondah, it's good to see you."

"It's good to be here Pastor. Thank you for the message this morning because I needed it. I wanted to apologize for the way I acted a few weeks ago. I was in a bad headspace and allowed the frustration of my situation to control how I reacted to it."

"Thank you for apologizing, however let me ask a question. You reacted to your situation, but how are you recovering from it? See, responding to a thing, that's easy. Recovering from it, that's work."

"I've chosen to recover, and it started by changing things in my life."

"You aren't leaving the church, are you?"

"Oh no. I love it here. I'm talking about physical and emotional changes."

"Good for you. If there's anything you need from me, you know how to reach me."

Chapter 39

"Wow, you look great." Denise says walking into the closet where I've been standing in front of the floor length mirror for fifteen minutes.

"You don't think it's too much for a hospital fundraiser?" I ask referring to the black, floor length, one shoulder evening gown.

"Girl, stop. Can't nobody wear their shoulder out like you." She laughs.

"What? I love my shoulders."

"Clearly. Seriously, you look amazing."

"As do the two of you." I touch her stomach.

"Ladies, it's time to go." Daniel hollers.

"I'm nervous." I admit grabbing my clutch and checking my hair and makeup.

"You've been out with Alonzo plenty of times."

"I know and each time I feel like this."

"Well, you look and smell great and your date is fine. No need to be nervous."

"Gee, thanks."

Daniel whistles when Denise and I step into the living room.

"Girl, if you weren't already knocked up, I'd get you pregnant tonight." He laughs reaching for Denise who swats him.

"I can't top that." Alonzo chuckles. "You look absolutely stunning."

"Thank you."

"Shall we go."

Walking into the Cadre Building downtown, Alonzo takes my hand. The entire building is decorated black and white with red hearts throughout. Music is playing, and people are everywhere. We stop and check in.

"Mrs. Jennings." Someone squeals.

I turn to see Harvey's assistant, Kendra. She rushes up, giving me a hug.

"You look amazing."

"Thank you. You look great yourself."

"I was sorry to hear about the divorce. That daggum Harvey is crazier than a redneck with an alligator to have let you go and I told him as much. And," she steps closer to whisper, "I didn't like the other gal. She was nasty. I told him that too. You could have bought me for a nickel size can of beer when I found out the baby wasn't his. Poor thang."

"Kendra, how have you been?" I ask to change the subject.

"Busy." She says cradling her stomach. "Baby number seven. I swear Jensen loves me pregnant, but after this he's getting his little fellow," she makes scissor gestures with her hand. "If you know what I mean. Shoot, I haven't had a hot girl summer in six years."

"Babe, I have our table number." Alonzo says recognizing my need to get away.

"Hi, I'm Kendra."

"Alonzo."

"Y'all make the cutest couple. Okay, gotta go. Bathroom break." She whispers before walking away waving.

"My ex-husband's assistant." I shake my head.

Daniel and Denise are sitting at a different table, so I head off to find our seats while Alonzo goes to the bar. The table is half full by the time I get there.

"Hello." I speak and sit.

"Hi, I'm Dr. Tracy Newman from LeBonheur and this is my husband Jordan."

"Hi, I'm Dr. Wondah Jennings."

"What hospital are you representing?"

"No hospital affiliation, I'm a marriage counselor who's here tonight with a friend."

"Oh, marriage counselor. Your job is harder than mine." She laughs.

"Sometimes." I look around for Alonzo when the lights dim, and everyone begins to clap. The lady on the microphone explains the reason for tonight's event and invites everyone to take advantage of the silent auction before introducing the band.

"Hey. Sorry, the line was long." Alonzo says handing me a drink.

"No problem."

"Would you like to dance?" he asks after chatting with a few people at the table.

"Sure."

The band plays "Let's Stay Together" by Al Greene. Alonzo sings in my ear and I smile. "Let me be the one you come running to. I'll never be untrue."

We stay on the floor until the music changes to "Just My Imagination" by The Temptations. Getting back to the table, the servers are preparing to serve dinner.

"I'll be right back."

Coming out of the bathroom, I see Harvey walking in my direction.

"Wondah, you look incredible."

"Thanks." I try to move pass him.

"I'm sorry. I've wanted to come by the house, Denise advised me to wait. Wondah, can we talk?"

I sigh, turning back to him. "Harvey, whatever you want to say, save it. I don't need to hear it and especially not here. Enjoy your night."

"You may not, however I need to say it. I set up an account with the florist to send flowers on our anniversary ten years ago. I gave them an idea on what I wanted the notes to say and they handled everything. After the divorce, I never got the chance to cancel it and I felt horrible when I realized what happened. The note, it was a song and somehow the person who typed it up, didn't finish the line. Wondah, I never lied about loving you. Yes, I handled things wrong, but love was never the issue. In fact, the song is by Michael Bolton and it says, said I loved you, but I lied cause this is more than love I feel inside. Said I loved you, but I was wrong cause love could never ever feel so strong."

"Are you done?"

"I'm sorry." He repeats.

"I've heard."

I walk off and leave him standing there.

Alonzo and I have a great time at the fundraiser. We stopped by IHOP for pancakes because the overpriced food had good intentions, bad taste. After saying our goodbyes, I walk into the house, arm the alarm and prepare to shower when the doorbell rings.

Opening the ring doorbell app, I roll my eyes when I see it's Harvey.

"Go home." I say through the app.

"Wondah, will you please give me five minutes of your time?"

"Sure."

I turn off the light in the living room and head for my bedroom.

Harvey can kiss my ass.

Chapter 40

Two weeks later, I'm standing amongst boxes in the home office. The offer I put on the house in Olive Branch, Mississippi was accepted last week and now it's moving time. Georgia says I should be able to close within thirty days and I've been praying things go smoothly so renovations can be done before my birthday.

Multiple offers were placed on this property for way over asking and after going through them, I finally settled on one. It's being presented to the couple today. If all goes well, I'll be closing this chapter and opening a new one within the same week.

Moving a box from the top of the closet, I look inside to see a picture of me and Harvey the day we moved in. I rub my hand across it before dropping it back in. I refuse to allow myself to travel back down the road of what was.

It's my past.

My watch dings with a reminder of the meeting with Dr. Holiday. I push some things from the desk and open my laptop, connecting to Zoom and waiting until she lets me into the room.

"Good afternoon Wondah, how are you?"

"I'm good Dr. Holiday. How are you?"

"Everything is well. How have things been since the last time we spoke? It's been a couple of months because you kept rescheduling the appointment. Why is that?"

"I had a lot going on and felt like I needed more time."

"How are things now?"

"Things have been, well, they're getting better."

"Better, implying they'd gotten worse?" she inquires.

"It depends on your definition of worse." I smirk.

"Wondah, let's cut the shit because you're skilled enough to know what I meant and maybe your time and life isn't valuable enough to not want to waste it, but mine is. I'm here for you because you came looking for a better way to manage the anger, stress and anxiety from the demise of your marriage. Is this still something you desire?"

"Yes, and I apologize if it seemed like this isn't important. Dr. Holiday, over the past month I forced myself to face some dark and lonely moments. It wasn't because no one was there for me, I realized there were some stuff I had to face alone."

"And what did you figure out?"

"I have to accept reality."

"Which is?" she asks.

"My marriage is over."

"Your marriage is over and it's okay." She adds. "Suddenly life as you know it can change and no matter how hard it is to accept and how much it hurts, sometimes we have to say okay. Not, okay it's whatever but okay, let me figure out how to deal with this and survive."

"Surviving got rough for a moment, I can't lie. There were times I questioned my sanity, like how did I not see this coming. I'd get up in the morning angry because I wasn't supposed to be divorced. This wasn't supposed to be my life, yet it was handed to me and I had no choice but to accept it because there was no return address. Instead of celebrating my fiftieth birthday, I was grieving a marriage I didn't even know was dying. Man," I wipe the tears. "I told myself I wouldn't cry today."

I drop my head into my hands.

"Whew." I exclaim while the wiped tears are replaced with fresh ones. "I know the divorce wasn't my fault. Yet, as I prepare to move to a new house and start over, there's still a sting of pain and regret."

"Why regret?"

"For the years wasted."

"Were they really wasted though? Before you answer, think about everything accomplished throughout your marriage. Your daughter, business, home, memories from vacations and etc. You didn't waste the years, you lived them."

"I guess I'm," I sigh.

"What?"

"The hardest part in all of this is seeing how easily Harvey could walk away. Him turning his back and acting like the past thirty years didn't exist hurt more than finding out about the affair. It's like we were a stain on his hand, easily washed off by soap and water and once it was gone, it was as if it never existed."

"Have you spoken to him?"

"Not in the way you recommended because I don't believe he deserves it. Why should I give him the benefit of having a conversation afterwards when it should have happened before?"

"Wondah, the conversation isn't to absolve him of wrongdoing or even to get an apology. I told you before, you don't require his approval to get closure. However, you need to close any gaps that may leave room for anger to fester because when there are spaces, the enemy will fill them. When you're laying awake at night and your mind is moving at rapid pace trying to figure out why, the enemy is sitting nearby waiting to use it against you. As long as you have questions, you'll also have anger and unresolved anger leads to resentment which then turns you bitter. How will you ever find love again when everything you'll produce going forward is from bitterness?"

"You're right however what do I do? I don't know if I can sit across from him and have an adult conversation. Dr. Holiday, this man hurt me, and I probably could have dealt with it better had he been honest. Now, each time I look at him I see a stranger who appears to be who I married twenty-eight years ago, yet it's hard to believe and accept anything he says."

"Here's what you do. Set a time and place of your choosing and take control. Don't allow him to pop up when it's convenient, control the situation because it's about you, not him. Ask questions if you want or don't however formulate your anger into words, holding nothing back and by the time it's over, leave there with your peace and the power to heal."

"Thank you, Dr. Holiday."

"Now, tell me something good that has happened since the divorce."

I tap my face with a Kleenex from the desk drawer. "I found a new house."

Chapter 41

I move around the patio lighting the torches and fire pit. I sit the bottle of bourbon and all my cigar essentials on the table, along with a blanket across the arm of the couch. Looking at my watch, my guest should be arriving any minute, so I take my phone and queue up the song, "Stranger in my House," by Tamia.

When I hear the gate to the backyard open. I press play.

"I don't understand, you look just like the man in the picture by our bed. The suspense is pounding and clouding up my head. I'm checking your clothes and you wear the same size shoe. You sleep in his spot and you're driving his car, but I don't know just who you are. There's a stranger in my house, it took a while to figure out. There's no way you could be who you say you are, you gotta be someone else."

I turn down the volume. "Harvey, thank you for coming. Please have a seat."

I sit, spread the blanket over my lap then I pour myself a drink, take a cutter and snip the end of my cigar. Flicking the torch, I light the end. Taking a long pull, I blow out the smoke.

"May I have a drink?" he asks.

"You may not, you won't be here long, and this isn't a cordial visit. I only have one question. Why the sudden divorce?"

"Wondah, we've been through this."

"Actually, we haven't. Please understand, you don't have to answer. I only thought we could have an amicable conversation." I mock, pulling on the cigar again.

"I've loved you since I was twenty years old. You were the one person I could tell my dreams to and you'd push me to make them a reality. When I said I wanted to be a doctor, you helped me research schools and you stayed up late to help me study."

"Can we skip the trip down memory lane? I know I'm a great woman, it still doesn't answer the question."

He looks out onto the lake.

"If you can't be answer, let's end this now."

"I wanted something different." He admits. "I was getting complacent in this life. I mean, we have everything we set out to get. We raised our daughter, built the house, paid it off in fifteen years and attained our career goals. We've taken the vacations and accomplished all we could together. I didn't think there was anything left for us."

"So, instead of talking to your wife, you go and have divorce papers drawn up because you got bored. Interesting. Was this before or after Anette."

"Anette had nothing to do with it."

"Sure. Okay. Thanks for coming."

"Wondah, I apologize for the way I handled this. The hardest part of all this has been Haven. I haven't spoken to her in almost two weeks and it's killing me."

"Haven? She's been the hardest part." I lay my cigar down and scoot to the edge of the couch. "You know what's been the hardest for me? Thinking I knew you. I mean, after all you were supposed to be my person for life and for a while, you were. You were who I came home to, talked about everything with, fell asleep next to for over thirty years, crafted dinner around your taste and shaved parts of me the way you liked even if I didn't.

I know your body better than I know my own, you've seen me at my lowest and highest and I've experienced more with you than I have my own family. You were one person I never considered betraying because then it would mean betraying myself, seeing we were intertwined. You were so deep within me that every time you took a breath, my lungs inhaled too. I never pictured a part of my life without you because I never thought I'd have too, not this soon. Yet, when that changed for you, you didn't even have the decency to tell me. Instead, you blindside me with a divorce on what should have been a happy day for me. Leaving me to figure out a way to remove the dark stain you left on my birth date."

"You're right."

"I know I am, but you want to know how I did it? By trying to cleanse you from my soul. So, I drank until I couldn't remember who I was or where I resided, and I lashed out at the people who were left to pull me out of the pit you suddenly and without warning shoved me into. I turned my back on God because I blamed Him when the truth is, I was the one wrong. I put you in control of my heart and instead of you giving it back when you were done, you crushed it. Did you even think of what this would do to me or did the need to get away overshadow your compassion for the woman you claimed to love?"

"Wondah, I do love you and when I played this out in my head, I thought you'd bounce back like you always do because you're this strong, dominant woman who I've seen overcome a lot. You help people and I assumed you'd be okay."

"You assumed?" I chuckle. "Yes, I help others but who in the hell did you think would help me? Did you ever stop to think the reason I was able to overcome some things because I had a husband I could lean on?"

"I handled things wrong and I'm sorry. I apologize for hurting you."

"Harvey, it's not just about hurting me because you were going to do that anyway, it's the way you left me. I wouldn't have stopped you from leaving, I couldn't have, but it didn't give you the right to wound me and then walk away. The least you could have done was ensure help could find me. Instead, you treated me like I was a squirrel you'd run over, leaving the remains of my body to be eaten by vultures."

He exhales. "You're right and I've apologized. I was wrong, how many other ways can I say it. I'm sorry and I pray you'll forgive me one day."

"I have forgiven you and this conversation wasn't to hear another apology. I don't need it and truthfully, it's not sincere. The purpose was to close spaces the anger of unanswered questions created. Harvey, I've spent this past year hating you and it did nothing to you. Anger kept me up questioning my identity and worth while you slept peacefully. So, tonight, I'm taking back my power by returning to you what was never mine to begin with."

"What's that?"

"The blame. You can have it because I'm done."

He stands. "Then I guess there's nothing else to say."

"There's one thing."

"What?" he inquires.

"Goodbye."

I give him the deuces before pressing play on the next song, "Goodbye" by Lionel Richie while sitting back and relighting my cigar.

I wanted you for life. You and me in the wind. I never thought there'd come a time that our story would end. It's hard to understand, but I guess I'll have to try. It's not easy to say goodbye."

He takes about a minute to gather himself and I watch him walk out the gate. When he does, I allow the tears to fall for what will be the last time over this.

Chapter 42

"Girl, this house is everything." Denise squeals walking in.

"I know, right. I love it. Be careful." I tell her when she bumps into something. "I don't need you falling over any of these boxes."

"How does it feel?"

I sigh and look around the living room. "Amazing."

"I'm proud of you."

"I'm proud of me too." I smile. "It took me a while, but I'm getting back to being happy and it feels great."

"Girl, what the hell you doing moving to the country?" Sharda screams coming in, bumping into a box. "I dang near ran out of gas trying to find a gas station. Out of all the houses in Memphis, you had to move your tail down here."

"Will you stop? This isn't the country and I love the neighborhood."

"Lies. I saw chickens in them folk yards across the street. We almost had one for dinner had he been a few seconds slower."

We laugh.

"Hush and come help me unpack the kitchen."

After getting the kitchen, living room and my bedroom cleaned up, Denise, Sharda and I order dinner in. We're sitting on the floor around our makeshift picnic.

"How was the conversation with Harvey?" Denise asks.

"It wasn't long, and it did exactly what I needed. Closed things."

"Did he tell you why the quick and abrupt divorce?"

"Yeah, he was bored."

"Hold on. I know you lying?" Sharda says.

I shrug. "He said we'd accomplished everything, and he didn't think there was anything else for us to do, together."

"Sis, I'm sorry." Denise rubs my leg.

"I'm good because it allows me to finally come to terms with this not being my fault."

"It was never your fault."

"I know, but when you're knee deep in anger and unexpected change like divorce, all kinds of things go through your mind. Yes, I know I'm a good woman, wife and mother, but baby darkness will have you seeing parts of you that don't exist. I questioned who I was as a woman because why else would a man leave a marriage after twenty-seven years."

"Stupidity."

"Thinking the grass is greener."

"Or, and I'm not taking up for bobblehead, but his mind could have made him actually believe his reasoning. Yet, it's his loss. In February, I was writing in my journal and it happened to be ten months since Harvey presented me with divorce papers. At first, I thought of it as a prison sentence, then the Holy Spirit said the ending of a pregnancy. Only this pregnancy didn't end with a happy healthy baby, although I had to go through the delivery. The Holy Spirit played for my remembrance, the nights of pain, the days of crying and the moments of being balled up in the floor screaming for God to make it end. I was angry at God for not allowing my baby, i.e. my marriage, to live when I had done everything right. I couldn't understand then God saying, to everything there is a season. Y'all, I sobbed for hours, letting the grief go then I got up."

"Good God." Denise cries.

Sharda opens her mouth.

"Don't you dare start singing." I tell her wiping tears before we burst into laughter.

Once Denise and Sharda are gone, I turn off the lights and arm the alarm. Walking pass the room I'm going to use as an office, I see a light.

"Now, I know—oh my God."

"Don't be afraid Wondah. God has heard your prayer."

"Oh, it's you." I roll my eyes. "Look, I apologize about our last, um, encounter but I was in a bad space mentally."

"I understand." He clasps his hands in front of him.

"So, what's the message? Is God still mad at me? Did He send you to punish me?"

"He was never upset with you Wondah. If He was, He could have easily shut your mouth like Zechariah or blinded you like Saul on Damascus Road. God simply needed you to trust Him. See, had He stepped in before, you could have said it was expertise in marriage counseling that pulled you through. If He would have showed up before, you could have taken credit for not losing your mind. Yet, in showing up after you'd counted yourself out, after you thought your identity in self was dead, after the drinking, after the nights of angry outbursts, the thoughts of suicide and thinking there was no hope; now you can trust in the power of God."

He walks closer to me.

"Wondah, you had to go through recovery in order to make it to restoration."

"Couldn't it have been an easier way?"

"Sure, but would you have appreciated your next without the struggle of the former? You thought your heart wouldn't recover after being crushed by man's actions, when man can't destroy the heart God created. All God has ever wanted was you, strong and with an identity. Through pain, you found your way back. You regretted the years as lost and I'm here to declare God's word from First Peter five, verses ten and eleven, "But may the God of all grace, who called us to His eternal glory by Christ Jesus, after you have suffered a while, perfect, establish, strengthen, and settle you. To Him be the glory and the dominion forever and ever. Amen."

"Amen. God, I thank you and thank you sir for being patient with me. I know I didn't give you the best welcome when it came to delivering God's word. Yet, I hear you."

"I'm used to it." He touches me and when I open my eyes, it's day out and I'm in my bed. I close my eyes and smile. "Amen."

Chapter 43

April 10, 2021

Today, I'm 50 + 1 years old. Man, what a year it's been. I finally closed on the sale of my old home and I must say, the selling price was pretty sweet. I'd planned to throw a party in my new house to celebrate making it. I wanted balloons, music, drinks and my family because I thought I needed to erase the stain of last year's pain. Then I realized, I didn't need a party. The one thing I needed more than anything was peace. So, I'm sitting out on my patio with a cigar and glass of bourbon.

Tonight, on my 51st birthday, I'm no longer sad (although there are still remnants of pain), I'm no longer wishing for what I used to have (although there were some great memories) and neither am I in a sunken place. I'm healing. I wish I could say I'm healed, but baby grief is a process and it takes time. A LOT OF TIME.

I ran into Harvey the other day at Lowe's while Alonzo and I were shopping for bathroom paint. No, he and I aren't in a "relationship," we're friends who are healing together and enjoying each other platonic company. Anyway, Harvey and I spoke in passing because we aren't on the level of any kind of conversation. Plus, the fact I didn't knock his ass upside the head with the can of Salty Dog Interior Paint I was holding is a clear indication of my healing.

Speaking of healing, I'm still in therapy with Dr. Holiday and the occasional class at Release. Those two things, along with God, my family and church are what keeps me sane.

"Mom, come on." Haven yells from the house.

"One second."

Haven is home for the weekend and we're going to watch a movie called The Quiet Place.

Until tomorrow.

I close my journal then my eyes.

"God, thank you for allowing me the chance to see a new day while celebrating another year of life. Please forgive me for the selfish moments I was angry at You for what wasn't your fault. Father forgive me for the minutes I took for granted. I can't say if I had to do it again, if I'd change anything because the suffering saved me. Although, I may not have understood it then, I'm thankful for it now. In the posture of pain was where I stopped neglecting praise.

It was rejection who taught me to rejoice in all things, hurt showed me healing and the fight taught me just how strong I was. It took losing my identity to identify who I am in you. Thank you, God. I know I screamed for you to make it stop, I lashed out when it got hard and I turned away when I couldn't understand; yet you never left. Thank you. Thank you for allowing the suffering because the suffering saved me. Oh, but Father, the next time there's something you need me to hear, see or learn, text me because there's got to be an easier way. Nonetheless, I trust you. Amen."

I open my eyes, inhaling and exhaling before getting the pen to make one last note.

I don't know what this new year will bring, however the last one tested my strength, faith and patience enough to know ... I can make it. Marriage didn't define me, and divorce didn't break me. It caused some bruises child, but they're healing and I'm getting back to happy.

Happy with who I am.

Wondah Renee Parker Jennings.

Happily single.

Thank you for taking the time to read Wondah. Although this is a fictional story, I pray something shared has helped you in some way. I've never gone through a divorce, yet I prayed for God to let me feel Wondah in order to reach the hearts of you who have. Many times, we carry the burden of someone else blame because we don't find a healthier way of coping with pain, anger, bitterness and loss. We tend to tug the heaviness of what they did, never fully healing only masking. We become great at covering up what we need to be released from.

Here's my prayer for you ... Lord, let my sister and/or brother fully heal, closing every wound inflicted by divorce, separation, abuse, cheating, abandonment, lies and unanswered questions of why. God, close every gap opened by grief, heal every hole of hate, restore what rejection removed, break away whatever bitterness built and redeem what divorce or breakup tried to take. God, my sister and brother deserve to feel genuine love again. They deserve happiness. They deserve to be healthy and whole. They deserve to be free of what has kept them bound. God, when they're ready, release them. While they thought they needed an apology and closure, let them see all they truly need is peace. Father, I pray the one who turned away from you will repent and seek you again. The one who closed off their heart to love, will try again. Father bless your people to know, they can find strength through the pain. Amen.

Also, I wouldn't be Lakisha if I didn't leave you with this. If you need help, get it. Seek a licensed therapist because therapy isn't a bad thing. You deserve to be healed, happy and whole. You deserve to be free. You deserve to be you.

Again, thank you for taking the time to read and support Wondah. This is my 30th release!! I pray you enjoyed it. If you did, please leave a review, post it on social media (tag me) and share it with friends and family. If you're a member of a book club and would like to feature this book, email me at authorlakisha@gmail.com as I'd love to be a part of the discussion.

If you're a cigar lover, please check out Chicks and Cigars (yes, it's a real thing) on IG or www.chicksandcigars.com. If you love candles, visit https://ruckercandles.com/

Again, and as always, I'm grateful each time you support me. If this is your first or twentieth time reading a book by me, THANK YOU! If we haven't connected on social media, what are you waiting for.

Twitter: _kishajohnson

Instagram: @kishajohnson and @DearSisVlog

Snapchat: Authorlakisha

Tik Tok: @AuthorLakisha

Email: authorlakisha@gmail.com

Please check out the many other books available by visiting my Amazon Page. For upcoming contests and give-a-ways, I invite you to like my Facebook page, AuthorLakisha, join my reading group Twins Write 2 or follow https://authorlakishajohnson.com/. You can also join my newsletter by clicking HERE.

About the Author

Lakisha has been writing since 2012 and has penned more than twenty-five novels, devotionals and journals. You can find topics of faith, abuse, marriage, love, loss, grief, losing hope etc. on the pages of her many books.

In addition to being a self-published author, she's also a wife of 22 years, mother of 2, Grammy to one, Co-Pastor of Macedonia MB Church in Hollywood, MS; Sr. Business Analyst with FedEx, Devotional Blogger, the product of a large family. She's a college graduate with 2 Associate Degrees in IT and a Bachelor of Science in Bible.

Lakisha writes from her heart and doesn't take the credit for what God does because if you were to strip away everything; you'd see Lakisha is simply a woman who boldly, unapologetically and gladly loves and works for God.

Ask her and she'll tell you, "It's not just writing, its ministry."

Also available

Pastor Layton and Lady Natasha Briggs were destined to marry. Well, according to their parents who arranged things before they were old enough to walk.

Now, thirteen years later, Layton and Tasha find themselves at odds. Love, honor and cherish have all been replaced with arguing, accusations, and domestic violence. A toxic environment that is tainting the heart and mind of their six-year-old daughter Lael.

Early one Sunday morning, things take a more violent turn, leaving Lael to make a 911 call that will chill the darkest of souls. Proverbs 18:22 says, "He who finds a wife finds a good thing and obtains favor from the Lord." But what happens when the love is lost and there are secrets behind closed doors?

Chance McGhee is a few months shy of her 40th birthday and marrying the man she's spent the last three years with until he dumps her two months before the wedding. Left devastated and angry, she prays telling God she'll remove her hand and wait for Him to give her another chance at love or she's done for good.

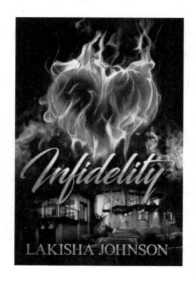

Lauren Daniels had everything planned. She'd go to college, get the degree, settle down, get married, build her career as a sought-after architect and have a family. For the most part, things worked accordingly. Until she decides to change the plans to get what she wants.

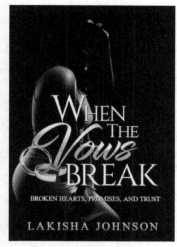

Dearly beloved, that's how it begins, what God has joined together, let no man put asunder; that's how it ends. Happily married, wedded bliss and with these rings, we do take; but what happens to happily ever after when the vows break?

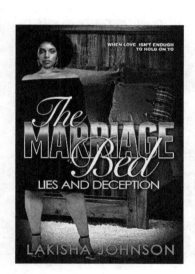

Lynn thinks their marriage bed is suffering. Jerome, on the other hand, thinks Lynn is overreacting. His thoughts, if it ain't broke, don't break it trying to fix it. Then something happens that shakes up the Watson household and secrets are revealed but the biggest secret, Jerome has, and his lips are sealed.

They say first comes love then comes ... a kidnapping, attacks, lies and affairs. Someone is out for blood but who, what, when and why? Secrets are revealed and Rylee fears for her life when all she ever wanted was not to be The Forgotten Wife.

What would you do if you woke up one morning with pain doctors couldn't diagnose, medicine couldn't minimize, sleep couldn't stop and kept getting worse?

Still Fighting is an inside look into my sister's continued fight with Trigeminal Neuralgia, a condition known as the Suicide Disease because of the lives it has taken.

Other Available Titles

A Compilation of Christian Stories: Box Set

Shattered Vows Box Set

Dear God: Hear My Prayer

2:32 AM: Losing My Faith in God

When the Vows Break 2

When the Vows Break 3

Shattered

Shattered 2

Tense

Broken

The Pastor's Admin

The Family that Lies

The Family that Lies: Merci Restored

Last Call

Covet

Chased

I'm Not Crazy

While I Slept

Bible Chicks: Book 2

Doses of Devotion

You Only Live Once: Youth Devotional

HERoine Addict – Journal

Be A Fighter - Journal

Surviving Me - Journal

CPSIA information can be obtained
at www.ICGtesting.com
Printed in the USA
BVHW041151090821
613997BV00015B/716

9 781087 980034